PUBLISHER INC.

ISBN 1-56315-155-3

Trade Paperback
© Copyright 1999 Esther Lakritz
All rights reserved
First Printing—1999
Library of Congress #98-87014

Request for information should be addressed to:

SterlingHouse Publisher, Inc.
The Sterling Building
440 Friday Road
Department T-101
Pittsburgh, PA 15209

Cover design: Lisa Galla - SterlingHouse Publisher
Typesetting: Steve Buckley

This is a work of Fiction. Names, characters, places, and incidents either are the
product of the author's imagination or are used fictitiously. Any resemblance
to actual events or persons, living or dead is entirely coincidental.

Printed in Canada

For Simeon who saved the day.

PROLOGUE

September 24, 1861

The pounding on the door continued without letup, rising to a crescendo.

"I'm going out there and talk to those men before they break the door down," Jenny said. "Todd, listen to me - you stay here. I'll try to reason with them."

"I wish you wouldn't," he said. He was still wearing the blue flannel shirt and gray pants from the day he deserted. "They're out there for blood. Can't you hear them? They won't listen to reason. Martha, talk to her."

His wife pleaded. "He's right, Jenny. I'm afraid you're going to get hurt. Don't go. There are rebels out there."

"How could that be? We're far from the war. The rebels wouldn't dare come north."

"They're vigilantes," Todd said. He looked through the scope of his rifle.

"Todd, don't shoot."

"Jenny, I have to protect my family."

"Todd, please, no. I beg you."

Jenny turned towards the staircase. Her heart thumped in her throat. Could she pull this off without any bloodshed? Would they listen to her? She stood before the door, pushing it slightly ajar, and slipped noiselessly outside.

Moonlight flooded the yard. There were three of them. They had tethered their horses to the single tree in front.

"Sheriff MacKenzie," Jenny said, "what are you doing here?"

"I might ask the same of you, Jennifer."

"I'm writing a feature story about Todd for the WASHINGTON

EVENING STAR."

"And I'm here to arrest Todd because he's a deserter."

"Sheriff, Todd and his wife think you're vigilantes and he feels he has to protect his family."

"I wonder if he knows deserters will be shot after they're brought to justice. Jennifer, do me a favor and move away from this area, over there to the side, just in case we have problems."

Then she saw the fourth horse, untethered, near the periphery of the yard. Where was the rider? A sudden movement caught her eye as a shadow detached itself from the tree.

The silhouette came forward in measured paces, a rifle in his hand. The long end of a white kerchief hung down over his shoulder. A signature? Union uniform? She squinted. Hard to tell. Confederate? This far north? She must be imagining things. A bandanna covered his face.

The voice was low, muffled. "Where's Todd?"

"Hey, what's going on over there?" the sheriff yelled. "Who is that guy?" More pounding on the door followed.

"I don't want to kill you, but I might have to, if you don't tell me the truth". He couldn't be talking to her.

She never saw this guy in her entire life. "Where's Todd," he asked again.

"He's in the house,:" Jenny said.

Jenny heard the sheriff holler. "Todd's got a gun."

The assailant raised his rifle. Jenny dropped to the ground before he fired. A woman screamed. Martha? The sheriff pounding on the door.

"Open up in the name of the law."

Jenny lay still. She raised her head, then pulled herself to a sitting position. A Confederate uniform hovered over her. The gunman got down on his haunches.

She tried to push him away. Her fingers coiled around a button on his jacket.

He slammed into her with such force that as she fell her hand ripped the button off. She tried to crawl away, but another blow crumpled her to the ground.

CHAPTER I

September 28, 1861

"Jenny, are you all right?"

She opened her eyes and saw a pert, copper haired girl whose freckled face would be identifiable anywhere. "Oh, Laura, what happened?"

"You had an accident."

"What kind of an accident."

"Don't you remember?"

"Afraid not."

"Someone hit you. We don't know why."

"Come on in," called Laura to the knock on the door.

"Dr. Fletcher."

"How's the patient today?" he asked.

"O.K., I think," Jenny said. "How long have I been here, Doctor?"

"Four days. I'm going to have to discharge you this afternoon because we need the space. You're in a military hospital. When you were brought in, we didn't have any place to put you so we converted this doctors' room for you."

"Who brought me here?"

"I don't know because I wasn't on duty. It was late at night so it must have been after the attack on you. That would be September 24. Then there were so many wounded being brought in, we just had to make room for you quickly."

Jenny moved her hand to her bandaged head. "Ouch."

"You sustained a blow to the head," the doctor explained,"and we had to cut some of your hair. You've had a concussion, Jenny, and will experience a short term memory loss as a result of your injury. You won't remember anything about your accident or the people involved. There will also be a problem recalling events immediately preceding the day before your accident. But anything that occurred three weeks before the attack, you'll be able to recall normally. Do you remember what kind of work you did long before the accident?"

"I'm a reporter for the *Washington Evening Star.*"

"Do you know who won the Battle of Bull Run?" asked the doctor.

"I guess I'll never forget that one - the Confederates. Will my memory ever come back?"

"In time," Dr. Fletcher said. "You must be patient. Don't try to force."

A knock on the door ushered in Sheriff MacKenzie. "Doctor, is it all right if I ask Jennifer a few questions?"

"Yes, but don't tire her. Jenny, I'll be back a little later to discharge you."

"How are you feeling, Jennifer?" the sheriff asked.

"All right, I guess. The doctor said I have a short term memory loss. Do you know what happened to me, Sheriff, and who brought me to the hospital?"

"I brought you to the hospital. As to what happened to you - I might be able to fill in a few of the missing blanks. I had gone to this home with two deputies to arrest a deserter."

"And I was there?" asked Jenny.

"Yes, Jennifer. You told me you were writing a feature story for the *Evening Star* about the family."

"I know I was working for the *Star*, but I didn't know until you just told me, why I was there at the scene of the attack."

"We pounded on the door and shouted up to Todd to come downstairs and open up. I looked in your direction. You were on the sidelines and I saw this guy stalking you."

"Do you know who he was?"

"I don't know his name, but I can tell you he's a Jessie Scout, unless he had disguised himself as one. You can always tell.

"They wear a Confederate uniform and they have this end of a white kerchief dangle over their shoulder. They're spies for the Feds. The Union soldiers don't bother them because that white scarf identifies them. When the Jessie Scout infiltrates the rebel lines, he removes the white scarf, ties it round his neck sometimes, and with his Confederate uniform he can move more freely in and out of Southern encampments."

"So you saw him strike me?"

"Oh yes, but there was so much confusion because Todd at that point had a rifle aimed at us, and then your assailant raised his gun, fired the first shot, killing Todd. He caught us off guard when he turned around and hauled off and swatted you.

"I heard you scream before you fell and ordered my deputy, 'Go get him', but it was too late. The assailant galloped away as if pursued by General Lee himself."

"Then you do think he was a Federal?"

"I don't know; I'm just guessing because he was wearing the Jessie Scout uniform."

"Sheriff, why did you have the murderer join you when you said you didn't know him?"

"I don't know him. Many times when my men and I would go after a deserter, we'd have the stray scout, like a Sheridan Scout or a Blazer Scout join our expedition. They hear about us and want to help. So when I saw this guy, this Jessie Scout, I thought nothing of it.

"By the way, Jennifer, when you were brought into the hospital, your hand still clasped this." The sheriff whipped out the button in his pocket. "Do you recognize it?"

"No."

"Apparently, when the assailant hovered over you and you tried to hold him back by pushing him away, your hand reached out and wrapped around his button on his jacket. Then when he smacked you so hard you fell forward, tearing the button right off the jacket."

"Is that button from a Confederate uniform?" Jenny asked.

"No doubt about it."

"Sheriff, do you have any idea why I was attacked?"

"That's what I'm trying to figure out. Do you know of anyone who holds a grudge against you?"

"No, and even if they did, why?"

"Something you wrote for your paper that angered them?"

"Can't think of anything."

"Then the only reason I think you were attacked is that the assailant did not want anyone to be able to identify him. He didn't expect to find anyone in that area and you probably took him by surprise. Then from there he was able to sneak up closer to take a shot at

Todd.

"For the time being, I won't bother you any more, but if you can remember something, anything about that night or the assailant, come to my office."

"Laura, what do you think of all that?"

"Scary. Jenny, I'm going to leave and let you rest a little before you're discharged."

Jenny wanted to say, "Don't go," but Laura left before she could raise her hand to detain her.

How will this memory loss affect her relations with those she knows? Jenny thought. At this stage, trying to piece together remnants as to what happened and why was hopeless. She wouldn't know where to begin. A knock on the door jolted her back to reality.

"Come in," she called.

"My child, how are you?" A priest entered the room and took her hand.

"Father, I'm not a Catholic."

"My dear child, that doesn't make any difference when it comes to consoling those who are in a hospital. I've been busy attending some of the soldiers, but when I heard about your mishap, I simply had to come to see how you were."

"Thank you, Father."

"Do you know who struck you?"

"No, I don't even know why I was attacked."

"So you wouldn't recognize your assailant if you saw him, say, in a police lineup." He came closer. His gray eyes were gunmetal, but his lips were saying something else.

"I wouldn't even recognize him if I saw him on a street corner. Father, do you know who hit me?"

"Of course not. I'll pray for you, my child." He waved to her as he opened the door and left.

A few minutes later Dr. Fletcher returned.

"Doctor, that was kind of you to send a priest to see me."

"What priest?"

"He left already."

"I never sent a priest to see you. As a matter of fact, if I knew that a priest were around here, I would have cornered him because a number of the soldiers out there are asking for one."

"The priest said he was attending some of the wounded."

"Couldn't be. I would have seen him. There was no one out there. You're sure he was a priest?"

"Of course I am. He was wearing the dog collar and a cassock."

"There must be some mistake because any priest that would be attending our men would be wearing the regimental blue of the Union Army and would have the chaplain insignia on his jacket. You're sure you weren't imagining or dreaming all this?"

"Positive."

"To get back to basics, Jenny, remember to take it slow and easy. Give yourself time, a lot of time, and you'll recover that portion of your memory that now seems to be a blur."

"All set to go?" Laura entered the room.

Jenny sat up in bed, ready to slip on her clothes.

"I'm going to take you to my home, Jenny. Your Aunt Irene hasn't returned as yet, so how about staying with me for awhile?"

As they left the hospital, Washington itself was far from reassuring. Heavy artillery was being dragged on stone boats pulled by oxen.

"Laura, what's going on?"

"The rebels are coming and we're all getting ready for a state of siege. You'll see forts erected everywhere in the city."

"Laura, I really should be home when Aunt Irene returns."

"I think you should stay with me," Laura said. "I'm sure you're a little woozy yet from your accident, a little unsteady on your feet, perhaps."

"I suppose you're right."

"Until you feel a little stronger."

"Laura, see that guy over there?"

"Where?"

"By the lamp post. He's been watching us. Oh, oh - he's coming this way."

"Would you mind getting out of our way, sir," Laura said.

"I want to talk to your friend."

"She doesn't want to talk to you."

"Can't she speak for herself?"

"I don't know you. Go away, please," Jenny said.

"Don't you recognize me at all?"

"As far as I'm concerned, I've never seen you before."

He looked at the bandage wrapped around her head.

"You're having a little memory problem, aren't you?"

"How did you know?"

"You just told me. Sometimes there are events in one's life that should as well be forgotten," he paused, "forever." With that, he turned on his heels and walked away.

"Oh, Laura, I wish I could remember what happened that night."

"You're much too hard on yourself."

"But at least I'd like to know who are my friends and who, my enemies."

"Jenny, you don't have any enemies."

As they neared Laura's home, Jenny saw the flag, torn and tattered, flying from a pole in the middle of the yard. She stiffened and felt her pulse quicken. A frisson of dread engulfed her.

"We decided to fly our flag," Laura said proudly, "and let the whole world know where we stand. Jenny, are you all right? You're trembling."

"Something in my memory...."

"Take it easy, Jenny. It's too bad that our Old Glory is so tattered, but it's the only one we have. Come on in the house and rest a bit and have a cup of tea, and we'll talk about the party I'm going to give."

"Let me stand here for a few seconds and see if I can bring up the image that my mind is struggling with."

Laura watched as a frown settled on Jenny's face. Jenny continued to stare at the flag as if hypnotized.

"Jenny," Laura said softly, afraid what was happening to her friend.

Jenny shook her head. "It's no use. Just can't. Whatever it is, it eludes me."

"Now, Jenny, don't protest, we're going to have a party to let our friends know you're out of the hospital and are much better. Nothing fancy, kind of an open house, but a few people, coming and going, some punch, very informal. Jenny, what's the matter?"

"I just can't seem to prod loose any thought, any notion, any visual impression of that night."

"Jenny, why worry? Everything will come back in time. The doctor said that, remember?"

"It's easy to say that and believe it, but it's frustrating to walk around in a fog."

"You're not being fair to yourself. You were just discharged from the hospital. Be patient."

"That flag - your flag. I'm sorry, but something jogged my memory. Something that frightens me."

"Where did you see a flag like this one? Here?"

"No, I don't know."

"That's the only flag we've ever had for many years. That's why it shows its age. Should really replace it."

"I feel like I'm searching through stacks and stacks of papers, riffling, shuffling them, but always moving blindly. It all seems so hopeless."

"Don't work too hard on it. It will come back."

"When? I can't go on like this the rest of my life. Every time something in my past turns up that will disturb me, what am I supposed to do? How am I to react?"

"Be patient with yourself. Don't forget what Dr. Fletcher said - that your short term memory loss should come back in a month or two. Come on, let's talk about the party."

"Laura, look at me. How can I go to a party? My hair has been cut. I have a black eye. My face is still swollen. All I want to do is go hide somewhere."

"Jenny, listen to me. You've been in the hospital for four days and a lot of people who care about you have been asking about you, want to know how you are. They know you've been through an ordeal. Besides, maybe someone will say something that might prove to be a clue to part of your missing memory.

"I suppose you're right."

"Besides," Laura said, "a party will do you a lot of good. For a couple of hours at least, you might forget about yourself."

Laura's mother was on the porch waving to them as the girls approached the house. Mrs. Martin's snow white hair and peaches and cream complexion were a stand-out in any crowd.

She hugged Jenny. "We're delighted to have you stay with us for awhile."

"Thank you," Jenny said.

"Honey, you don't have to thank me. You're almost like family. What's your Aunt Irene up to these days?" asked Mrs. Martin. "I miss seeing her."

"She's working with a group of Southern ladies trying to get control of Mount Vernon."

"Whatever for?" Mrs. Martin asked.

"They feel the Northerners can't care for George Washington's home like only the South can."

"So Irene hasn't changed much, has she?" Mrs. Martin smiled.

"Not at all," said Jenny. "She still believes that every Confederate is worth three Yankees."

"When is she returning to D.C.?"

"It might be a while yet. Quite a few of the Southern ladies invited her to stop over at their homes."

"Well, despite her politics, I like your aunt," Mrs. Martin said.

"Mother," Laura said, "I'm trying to convince Jenny about the party you and I planned."

"Oh yes, Jenny, by all means, you must. Come into the house and rest and have a cup of tea, and we'll talk about it," said Mrs. Martin.

"Laura, what can I possibly wear? I have nothing to wear. All my clothes are at home."

"Never mind. I don't want you running home for now. I have a pretty dress for you, Jenny, and I know it will fit."

"What can you do about my swollen face?"

"Don't worry about that. Even with a swollen face, you'll still be gorgeous."

"Laura, how did you get people to come on such short notice?"

"That was the easy part. The party has been in the planning stage the day before your discharge. Dr. Fletcher had given me an inkling when that would occur."

"What was the hard part?"

"Trying to persuade you to come."

The dress was pale blue broadcloth, trimmed with point lace that peeked out from the sweetheart neckline.

"Jenny, you're still the Jenny I know with your corn silk hair, even though it's clipped short, and your cornflower blue eyes."

"Laura, you didn't tell me who's coming."

"I want this all to be a surprise."

"If I don't remember anyone, it will be a surprise in more ways than one."

"Most of these people you know because you were acquainted with them long before your accident," said Laura.

The guests began arriving at 7:00 pm. Jenny saw his back first:

there was no mistaking that athletic build, even though he wasn't in uniform. It was the way he towered over everyone else; 6'4" he once told her. He turned his tanned, weatherbeaten face in her direction, as his blue-gray eyes swept the room, not missing any detail. The 60 year old lines around his eyes crinkled up as he smiled at her.

"Sher..." she began.

He placed a finger over his lips.

"Are you here for business or pleasure?" Jenny asked.

"I wanted to see how you were doing," Sheriff MacKenzie said, "and also, I thought, maybe, just maybe, the assailant might drop in to make sure that your memory hasn't returned.

"I'm here in my full capacity, just not in uniform, but don't let it get around." He winked at her.

Out of the corner of her eye, Jenny caught a flash of bright red pantaloons, blue tunic, and white leggings. He carried a silver mounted walking stick; on his hands were kid gloves.

He didn't give her a chance to say a word, as he reached for her hand and planted a kiss on it. "I missed you, chérie."

Jenny blinked, uncomprehending. "I don't understand."

"At the wedding."

"Whose?"

"Ours, ma chére."

"I'm sorry, but I have trouble remembering."

"Maybe next time." He laughed. "Au revoir." The Frenchman with the black curly hair and the well- trimmed sideburns and beard walked away and out of the house.

"Laura, did you hear that? Who was that?"

"I don't know who he is and I don't know how he got to the party because I know the people I had invited and a Zouave was not on my list."

"Then I wasn't going to marry him?"

"Of course not. That's just a line. I wonder why he came here. More important - how did he know you were here?"

"Jennifer," Sheriff MacKenzie walked to her side, "ever see that guy before?"

"Never."

"We'll probably never see him again, either," the sheriff said. "New York's 11th had a Zouave group to fight the rebels. Even if I wanted to find out who he is from the officer in charge, I don't know his name, so my query would be pointless."

"Laura, I think I'll sit over there on the sidelines," Jenny said. "Didn't realize how tired I am."

"Thought so," said Laura.

Jenny looked around the room. It was a happy time. A steady stream of friends walked by to shake her hand and wish her well.

"Remember me?" He was tall, sandy haired, and clean-shaven.

"How could I ever forget you, Bert?"

"Then your memory is back."

"Not really. The doctor said I'd experience a short term memory loss which meant the day of the attack and a few days before it. But after all, Bert, we met July 21st. I'd never forget a day like that."

"You almost killed me," he said gravely, but there was a twinkle in his eye.

"Not quite."

"Can I get you some punch?"

"Please."

"I'll be right back."

She'd never forget July 21st. That was a great and glorious day for a picnic and a lot of other people including Laura and her thought so, too.

"My mother insisted I take the buckboard," Laura had said. "She thought it was less dangerous."

"I heard that all of Washington's French cooks and hotelkeepers have tripled the prices of wine today and the hampers full of picnic provisions," Jenny said. "I'm glad I could pack my own lunch."

"Me too," said Laura.

"This is going to be the greatest sporting event of the season," said Jenny.

"Our next door neighbor told my mother," Laura had said, "the whole war will be over in 30 minutes, maybe an hour, the most."

"How does he know?"

"His guess is as good as anybody's."

"Where's your mother?"

"She's at home."

"Is she ill?"

"No. She can't stand all that shooting. Hurts her ears. Are you going to do a feature on the battle, Jenny?"

"No. My paper has the battlefield crawling with war correspondents. My editor wants me to do a story on the spectators."

"You mean like Senator Chandler? Did you see him marching in the parade?"

"Yes, and with that big Navy revolver strapped to that enormous stomach of his and he was huffing and puffing trying to keep up with everybody."

The battle had been raging for some time when they finally arrived at a good vantage point to observe it. First, they spread the contents of their picnic baskets on a red and white checked tablecloth that Laura had brought with her.

"Can you see anything at all?" Jenny asked Laura, who was looking through her opera glasses.

"White flashes like lightning. I can hear them, so it must be our artillery."

Jenny and Laura finished their lunch and ambled over to where most of the crowd was standing at Stone Bridge. Beneath it flowed the stream, Bull Run.

There wasn't much to see, Jenny noted. The battlefield was covered with dust and smoke. A shell ripped through the underbrush, spraying them with dirt and debris. They turned their heads, covering their faces with their hands.

From the grimy haze, like the genie in Aladdin's lamp, the kepi covered head of a Union soldier appeared. "You girls better be careful," he warned. "There are some shells the Confederates buried in these parts and those shells could explode at the slightest agitation."

"Laura, let's get out of here," Jenny said. The bursts of artillery and blasts of cannonade seemed to reach a new crescendo as Jenny and Laura threaded their way back to their wagon. Getting past the bridge slowed their progress because of the clot of spectators there still gaping at the battle.

"Let's go back to Washington," Jenny said, relieved they had made it safely to the buckboard. This is a real battle, not a dress rehearsal, thought Jenny.

Laura nodded in agreement and urged her horse forward. A cannon roared somewhere close by, then boomed as it found its mark. Artillery fire followed in rapid succession, adding to the clamor. Jenny put her hands over her ears.

"Your mother was smart to stay home," she said.

"Jenny, get down," Laura screamed, as the two women crouched low into the wagon. Their terrified horse reared up on his hind legs, then plunged earthward, almost dumping them on the ground and turning over the wagon.

A Union soldier fleeing from the battle area saw what had happened, ran over, and tried to calm the animal. The girls were effusive in their thanks.

"Much as I want to stop and get acquainted, ladies, I don't have the time. I've got to file my story before everyone else scoops me," he said.

"I thought you were a soldier with that uniform," Jenny said.

"Fat chance, that. Look, Miss, could I borrow your horse and wagon?"

"No," said Jenny. "Then we'll be stranded and how will we ever get back home?"

"You don't understand. I'm a correspondent with the *New York Herald* and there are 150 or more war correspondents out there in the field, all after the same story. The war's over, ladies; I got to get my story filed first and scoop everybody. There's a telegraph office in Warrenton."
He moved toward them. "Come on, give me a break."

"How did you get here anyway?" asked Laura. "You must have had some kind of transportation."

"I did, but my horse bolted and ran away. The noise of the cannon must have scared him off. So what do you say?"

"No," yelled Jenny.

"Yes," he retorted. He moved toward them and grabbed the side of the wagon, stepping on the wheel to boost himself up and over into the wagon.

"Laura, take the reins, get started - quick!" Jenny watched with horror as he placed one leg on the rim of the wagon wheel.

"Laura, go!" The stranger held on, but when the wagon started with a jerk he lost his grip, toppling from his perch, ending up in a crumpled heap on the ground.

"Laura, stop. Look! What are we going to do now?"
Both girls dropped to the ground and kneeled before the fallen man.

"Do you think he's dead?"

"I don't know. How could that be anyway?"

"Maybe when he fell he hit his head."

"He's lying very still."

"Jenny, we're going to have to get him to a doctor."

"How? We can't lift him."

"What can we do now?"

A piercing shriek shattered what had suddenly been a lull in the battle and bedlam broke loose as the picnickers near the Stone Bridge area ran towards them.

"Sir, could you help us, please?" Jenny asked a fleeing man.

"Make it quick. I've got a story to file for the *New York Tribune.*"

"We hava a man here, he's been hurt, and we want to lift him into the wagon."

"You'll have to help, too. The war's over ladies. I knew it wouldn't last once we got Beauregard stopped, pushed him right up against the wall."

"Who won?" Jenny asked.

He looked at her. "Are you kidding?"

"No."

"We won."

"You mean the North? The Federals? Us?"

"Who else? That's why I got to file my story, get it over the wire before anyone else beats me to it. What a great story. The war's all over now. Hey, what happened to this guy?"

"He fell off our wagon."

"I know him. That's Bert Wells from the the *New York Herald.* Ya-hoo, this is one time I'm going to scoop this bastard. Where are you two headed?"

"Back to Washington."

"With this crowd clogging the roads, I think I'd better head for Warrenton and beat the rest of these guys. You don't mind my hitching a ride with you, do you?"

"Not at all. It's the least we can do for you."

From Warrenton the girls went on to Washington.

"Where are we going to take this guy Bert Wells?" Laura asked Jenny.

"To Dr. Higginbotham. He's our family doctor." The doctor helped them carry the patient into his office. He asked no questions about the wound.

"I'll cleanse the abrasions on his leg," the doctor said, "and let him rest here for awhile. I think he's just dazed. He must have hit his head on a stone or something because he's really knocked out, but I don't think it's too serious," the doctor said, as he examined the head to see if there were any punctures. "Then he'll be free to go."

Much later, newsboys on street corners were hawking the latest edition with stories about the end of the war and how the North had put the South out of commission forever.

"Jenny, what's the matter? Are you O.K.?"

"What? Oh." Jenny looked into the concerned face of Bert Wells.

"What are you thinking about, Jenny?"

"Just reminiscing."

"You were a million miles away. Here's your punch. Sorry I was delayed. I had no idea there were so many members of the press here and of course we all had to stop and swap stories."

"What did they have to say?" asked Jenny.

"They all talked about the consequences they had to pay for filing an incorrect story."

"You mean like the North won the Battle of Bull Run?"

"A couple of the guys got canned."

Jenny gave him a sly smile. "And?"

"And I told them if it hadn't been for you, I'd probably be out of a job myself. You were bound and determined to keep me from climbing into that wagon. You did everything short of pushing me off, but I've got to thank you for that. Because of the accident, I didn't file that story of a Union victory.

"You saved my day and you saved my job. I can't forget that. If I had been stupid enough to file my original story, I know I'd be on the outside looking in all because everyone was in a hurry to get the story of a victory and outscoop everyone else and didn't bother waiting for the end of the battle."

"Hey, Carmie, over here. I'd like you to meet someone."
Jenny saw him approach and said under her breath, "Why couldn't he at least comb his hair? Looks like he slept in his clothes, too."

"Quiet," Bert whispered. "The guy's got a lot of clout."

"Jenny, this is James Carmichael. Carmie, do you know Jennifer Edwards of the *Washington Evening Star*?"

"Now I do." He smiled at her. "Are you a war correspondent, too?" he asked.

"Not really."

"Looks like you were in the war with that bandage on your head, the black eye, and swollen face. Weren't you?"

"Not quite." Thanks for calling attention to my appearance, she thought. "She was doing a feature about a deserter and his family and was the target of an unwarranted attack," Bert explained.

"By the deserter?"

"No, by an assailant."

"I am indeed sorry about that," Carmichael said, taking her hand. "I work for the *Philadelphia Enquirer*, and my editor shies away from giving out an assignment that will put his journalists in danger."

"Carmie, how did you get invited to this party? I thought the only people invited were friends of Jenny's."

"Well, I'm one now."

"You didn't answer my question, Carmie: who invited you?" asked Bert.

"A friend of a friend of a friend of Jennifer's. May I call you Jenny?"

"Of course."

"And you can call me Carmie."

"You sure get around," Bert said.

"That, my friend, is the understatement of the year."

"Carmie, I forgot to congratulate you on the successful gentleman's agreement you reached with General McClellan,"

"Yeah, it was tough going at times until I hammered it through. I hope that my colleagues will cooperate on this."

"A gentleman's agreement?" asked Jenny. "Carmie, don't the ladies count?"

"Of course, they do, my dear. The agreement is so simple it's a wonder with all the antagonism at my back that I could even push it through."

"Carmie," Jenny said, "does that mean there'll be more pressure on reporters as they gather the news?"

"That depends on the journalist. If he's going to write a story that he knows will help the enemy, he'll be in trouble."

"Is there a quid pro quo in this agreement?" Bert asked.

"You bet there is. The gentleman's agreement stipulates that reporters agree to refrain from publishing any matter that gives aid or comfort to the enemy. In return, McClellan promised he would ease the way for the press to get and transmit all information suitable for publication, particularly that which deals with engagements with the enemy."

"Sounds good. I hope it works," said Bert.

"There have already been problems. We are now censored by the

State Department, but sometimes it has been the War Department, and a few times the Treasury Department."

"Looks like the right hand doesn't know what the left hand is doing," said Bert.

"Exactly."

"So what's the solution?" asked Jenny.

"There has to be some uniformity or consistency because each one of these departments has a different idea how censorship should be run. These issues are yet to be ironed out."

"Carmie, can I talk to you?" One of the guests was pulling him away and towards the center of the room.

"Jenny," yelled Carmie, "any time you need help on this problem, let me know."

"Talk about conceit," Jenny said.

"Oh, I don't know about that," Bert replied. "He didn't tell you he just happens to be the chief Washington correspondent for the *Philadelphia Enquirer*. That shows you he's a modest, unassuming guy. Whatever you might think about Carmie, he's one guy who can out-scoop us all."

"Is that his claim to fame?"

"All I can say is that he finds scoops in the most unlikely places where none of us would dream or care to venture."

"Maybe, but his reputation precedes him, too, Bert."

"Really?"

"You mean you don't know? As an operator and a manipulator."

"So what? If he gets the news, that's the name of the game."

"What about ethics?"

"How do you spell that? Jenny, wake up. We're living in a cruel world."

"Sorry, I don't buy that."

"Too bad."

"Now I can understand," said Jenny, "why suddenly McClellan is portrayed in the *Enquirer* as a conquering hero in articles bylined by James Carmichael."

"I thought McClellan was described as a young Napoleon," said Bert.

"Whatever you want to call it, it's all puffery, as far as I'm concerned, and with an ulterior motive."

The evening soon drew to a close as guests filed past Jenny offering wishes for a speedy convalescence.

"Thanks for coming everyone," she said.

"Bert, aren't you leaving?" asked Jenny.

"Not yet. Are you going to show me the door?"

"Should I?"

"I want to get something settled."

"What?"

"When are you and I going to get together?"

"As colleagues?"

"No, as a couple."

"Bert, nothing could be farthest from my mind at the moment."

"Well, thanks a lot."

"I want to try to recover that lost part of my memory."

"What do you have to do for that - study, rest, or what?"

"I don't know. There have been times when I've encountered something, a simple object, like a flag flying from a flagpole and I become very frightened."

"Why?"

"I don't know. My memory during those times struggles to reach out and capture an image, as ill defined as it is, but fails me in coming to terms with reality."

"If there's anything I can do to help, I hope you'll call on me."

"Thanks, Bert, but I don't think anyone can help me, except myself. Sometimes I feel overcome with a great sense of guilt."

"How could that be? You were attacked! That just doesn't make any sense to me."

"It doesn't make any sense to me, either. Why should I have guilt? I didn't hurt anyone."

"In time, I'm sure, your questions will all be answered."

"I hope so," exclaimed Jenny. "Laura, have you been hiding?"

"Behind the punch bowl. Didn't you see me?"

"I think this was a very successful party, don't you? Where's your mother? I haven't seen her either the entire evening."

"She's in the kitchen."

"All this time?"

"Yup. She wanted to make hereself scarce - it was your party. I'm glad you enjoyed yourself."

"You were right, Laura. I did relax and forget about my problems."

"Well, ladies, I think I'll get going," Bert said. "Nothing more here for me to do. Take care, Jenny - I'll be seeing you."

CHAPTER II
September 29, 1861

Jenny woke to the wafting aroma of freshly baked bread. For a minute she forgot where she was. Then she remembered: Laura's house, of course. She dressed quickly and went downstairs.

"I've got buckwheat pancakes for you, Jenny," Mrs. Martin said.

"My favorite breakfast."

"Laura," Jenny said, "I think I'll visit Charlotte today."

"You just saw her a few days ago."

"I don't remember."

"It was the day before your accident, September 23rd."

"I'm sure Char is short of some things."

"Like what?"

"She can always use needles and thread. I've got a little box of tea and a small amount of sugar I think she would appreciate. Oh yes, and corset stays, too. I must have forgotten to give her some of these items last time I saw her because I found them in my reticule."

"And you're going to transport these across the border?" Laura asked.

"That could be dangerous," Mrs. Martin said. "Jenny, here are your pancakes and the syrup. Laura, could you pour the coffee, please?"

"Laura," Jenny said, "you make it sound like I'm traveling 40 days and 40 nights when Char lives just over the border."

"I'm worried about you," Laura said. "There are Confederate soldiers just 'over the border', as you describe it. What will you do when they stop you?"

"Why would they be interested in my needles and corset stays?

Who's going to think I'm a spy?"

"Jenny," Mrs. Martin said, "I'll be worried about you, too, until I know you're back here safe and sound. Why don't you encourage Charlotte to come north for the duration?"

"She's quite adamant about that."

"I think it's dangerous to scoot over the border like this," Mrs. Martin said.

"Jenny," Laura said, "don't forget that Virginia is the center of the Confederacy. Can't you mail her a few of these things?"

"No. My package would be too bulky. I'm bringing her a couple of Northern newspapers, too. That could be a problem if I tried to mail them. I know the post office would confiscate the newspapers, so I think I'll take my chance.

"Oh, I almost forgot about my horse," Jenny said.

"It's here in our barn with mine."

"Laura, you're a dear."

"When you were taken to the hospital, we didn't know how long your stay would be so my mother and I drove up to your house in the buckboard and I rode your horse back."

"Be careful, Jenny," Mrs. Martin called.

Laura and her mother stood in the doorway, watching Jenny mount her horse, wave, and gallop away.

"Jenny's brave, a lot braver than I could be," Laura said.

"Brave, maybe, but foolhardy. Takes too many chances. After all, we're in the midst of a war. So many unexpected things can happen. I'll be glad when she's back."

Jenny had always admired the countryside when she'd ride over to visit with Charlotte, but this time her eyes hungrily devoured every detail, etching it well in her memory, as if she would never see such serenity again.

Little lanes, ravines, and patches of woods dotted the landscape, untouched yet by the ravages of the battlefield. She shuddered as she tried to visualize how this peaceful rural scene would be violated eventually by the war.

Cedar and oak trees laying on their sides with gaping holes in their trunks were scarred forever. She imagined women and children also scarred, perhaps forever, clogging the roads with their life's possessions piled high, in wagons or on foot, terrified by the sounds of war in their desperate attempt to flee.

She shook off the effects of her own self-imposed nightmare and rounded the bend in the road, and there in a cul-de-sac stood the school-house.

It was still undamaged, and so was the flagpole in the front, its Stars and Bars flying high, but tattered and torn, almost in streamers, a badge of defiance.

She stopped, as a flood of memories overflowed in her. She seemed to float in time between yesterday and today. Something was coming to the surface as she continued to stare at the flagpole.

Then she remembered:

It was the day before her recent attack. She had come to visit her sister to persuade her to come north for the duration. School was in session then and Jenny had entered the classroom and watched as her sister spoke to the ten children assembled there.

"This will probably be our last class," Charlotte had said, "for a long time to come. Let's begin today's lesson with the assigned text for the morning, the 8th verse of the 6th chapter of Matthew. Jolene, can you recite the verse for today?"

The eighth grader rose. "Be ye not therefore like unto them; for your Father knoweth what things ye have need of before ye ask Him." Charlotte nodded her approval and the student sat down.

"All right now," Charlotte said, "let's proceed with today's spelling assignment. Garrett, stand, please." The 13 year old rose uncertainly from his seat, looking nervously around him for support.

"Garrett, spell the word 'medicine' for us."
The silence in the room was palpable.

"Garrett, speak up, please."

"Miss Charlotte," the boy began, shifting his weight from one foot to another, "Miss Charlotte," he began again, "I didn't study today's lesson." He dropped his head on his chest, waiting for the reprimand.

"Look at me, Garrett." Slowly, the boy lifted his eyes. "Yes, ma'am."

"I'm not going to punish you. Your punishment is severe as it is. Perhaps some day you'll appreciate what having an education means," Charlotte sighed resignedly, "when it's too late. With the war beginning, who knows when we'll ever have class again. You're the one I fear for, Garrett; you've never learned to spell properly. If the Yankees should win, what will happen to you, to your schooling?"

"I'm sorry, ma'am," Garrett said contritely.

"No, Garrett, I'm the one who's sorry...sorry for you

"You may be seated."

"Yes, ma'am."

"Is there anyone here who can spell the word 'medicine' correctly?"

A dark haired girl raised her hand. "All right, Jolene," Charlotte said, nodding her head in the student's direction.

Charlotte went to the board to write the word as Jolene began to spell, "M-E-D-I..."

A burst of gunfire interrupted the recitation. Charlotte whirled around, facing the class. The children had run to the window.

"Children, get down," Charlotte commanded. Everyone ducked below the window level.

The gunfire stopped as suddenly as it had begun. The children rose cautiously and peered through the windows. Jenny joined them, standing next to her sister.

There was the dull roar of a mortar shell somewhere in the distance. The crack of a rifle pierced the air followed by the pounding hooves of horses and five Federals rode into the schoolyard. With them, was a Confederate soldier, a white kerchief with its long end trailing over his shoulder.

The women stared in disbelief when he gave a blood-curdling yell, dismounted, and shinnied up the flagpole. The Union soldiers cheered him on as he reached upwards towards the flag. He took out a knife and in savage downward thrusts, he commenced his crusade to rip and mutilate.

Jenny looked at Charlotte who mirrored her fright.

"Jenny, can you hear me? Jenny, what's the matter? Aren't you going to come in to visit?" Charlotte broke into her reverie. She was standing on the steps of the school.

"I was just reliving that terrible day here when we feared the soldiers were going to storm the school."

"I've tried to forget that," said Charlotte.

"Unbelievable the way that flag triggered all those memories again for me," said Jenny.

"Come on in. There's no school."

"What are you doing then?" Jenny asked.

"Just cleaning up and removing some of the books. No one knows when school will open again and our lives will return to normal."

"Char, I wish you'd come north, for your own safety."

"I can't. If Brad is discharged, I want to be here waiting for him. Going north for me is like running away and I can't do that."

"I brought some stuff I thought you might be able to use. Northern newspapers like the *New York Tribune* and the *Washington Evening Star.*

"Naturally." Charlotte smiled.

"Also, some needles and thread, tea and sugar. I forgot to give you these last time I was here."

"You're spoiling me, Jenny."

"And corset stays."

"Jenny, you're a darling. How did you ever guess I desperately needed them?"

"What are you doing for substitutes?"

"Most of us around here are using wooden splits and the splits are made from white oak, but a friend of mine told me she preferred hickory. A lot of my own stays I removed from old corsets.

"But tell me, Jenny - is the sheriff any closer to finding who had attacked you? Your letter didn't give any particulars except the bare facts. I'm assuming that the investigation is ongoing."

"Yes, the sheriff is still working on the case. Sometimes I wonder if the assailant will ever be found."

"But what about you, Jenny? How do you feel? Have you regained some of your missing memory?"

"I feel fine; a lot better than the day following the attack. My short term memory loss is still unpredictable. That's why I had stopped in the school yard when I saw the flagpole with the same Confederate flag from that day of infamy. It was like a door had opened somewhere in my mind and I was reliving every single detail of that day from your chiding Garrett for not knowing how to spell to the Confederate who climbed the pole to hack at the flag as the ultimate outrage."

"Do you remember any details at all about your life?"

"I know who I am and that I'm a journalist with the *Washington Evening Star*, but all details of the assault and events of a few days before I draw nothing but a blank. Trying to weave together my life from the broken threads I know makes me feel lost at times."

"I'm so thankful you're just alive, dear sister."Charlotte hugged Jenny. "What does the doctor say? Is there hope you'll get your memory back?"

"Yes, but it will take time. Well, today, I got a little part back. Char, do you recall that Confederate soldier who had climbed the pole and tried to destroy the flag?"

"I'll never forget him. What about him?"

"He was not a real, genuine Southerner."

"I can believe that. So who is he?"

"I don't know his name. I was told he's a Jessie Scout. The sheriff told me that Jessie Scouts are Federals wearing Confederate uniforms. The peculiar way they display that white kerchief over their shoulder is their idientification. They are recognized by other Federals."

"I thought it odd, too, that the Confederate seemed to mix so well with the Union soldiers."

"Wearing the butternut, they can infiltrate among Southern lines, spy, and then come back and report to a Union officer. They tie the kerchief around their neck so it won't be so obvious when they enter the South. But this Jessie Scout wore the kerchief correctly. He probably felt he had nothing to fear accompanied by those Federals."

"Jenny, didn't you write in your letter that the sheriff said your assailant was a Jessie Scout?"

"That's right."

"Do you think the guy who slashed at our flag is the same one who struck you?"

"Could be; but who knows where he is now? Besides, there are a lot of Jessie Scouts around, especially in the Shenandoah Valley."

"I still don't understand, Jenny, why, he, whoever he was, attacked you?"

"I think and so does the sheriff that he didn't want me to identify him."

"He didn't want you to identify him as the murderer of Todd?"

"Right."

" Jenny, why did he kill Todd?"

"I don't know."

"Well, Jenny, as much as I would like to see him captured, I'm glad he's not in the area so as to cause you more problems." Charlotte placed a cup of tea in front of her sister.

"Char, I brought the tea for you and you alone and I feel guilty about drinking up your meager supply."

"You can bring me some more tea on your next trip. This tea tastes so good," Charlotte said after a sip.

"Too bad I didn't bring some cookies to eat with it."

"That's not important, Jenny. What's important isI have the tea. You have no idea how we're beginning to feel the pinch of the blockade."

"Anything else you'd like me to bring you on my next visit?"

"Fruits and vegetables, maybe. Oh yes, another pair of shoes. You know my size. Any color."

"I'll see what I can do."

"Jenny, I can't believe that the United States would cut off so many lifelines to the South."

"Char, don't forget the Confederacy started this war. The United States doesn't want to lose the South as part of its country."

"Yes, I know."

"There will be a lot more hardship in the future as the blockade tightens considerably and reaches a momentum," said Jenny.

"Do you think Lincoln might let up a little when he sees how the civilians are suffering as the war drags on, which I'm sure it will."

"President Lincoln won't loosen or stop the blockade until the South surrenders."

"You're sure about that?" asked Charlotte.

"That's the talk in Washington."

"Jenny, as much as I love having you visit, I think you should start back for home."

"Have there been problems in this area?"

"Problems, yes, and sometimes I feel a tragedy waiting to happen."

"Char, you didn't tell me."

"There have been marauding parties of Federals."

"You haven't been threatened, have you?"

"Not personally, no."

"That's O.K., then."

"No, it's not. They are a menace."

"In what way?"

"They told me they're going to burn down the school."

"Char, I had no idea!"

"I didn't want to tell you because I didn't want you to worry."

"Char, I want you to tell me! I want to know how you're coping. How many Feds usually come to bother you?"

"At the moment, it's only a party of six. Last time they were here they tried to remove the flag, but they couldn't because it's all in shreds and streamers."

"Do they speak to you?"

"Oh yes."

"How do you handle it?"

"I put on my best Southern accent. If I used my regular Yankee speech, they'd tar and feather me, I'm sure, as a Confederate sympathizer. So far my act works."

"Can the mail still get through?"

"Up to now."

"Write me if you're having troubles."

"Bye for now, Char. Take care."

"You, too, Jenny."

The girls embraced.

Jenny mounted her horse, waved to Charlotte, and glanced back at the flagpole one more time.

She hadn't told Charlotte about the fear that would sweep over her occasionally, the source of which she didn't know. She didn't want to unduly alarm her sister.

Whatever trauma she experienced that night of her attack continued to bedevil her. She must find any common strands among the clues that will emerge, like today when she could go back to the earlier visit with Char and recall that Jessie Scout defacing the flag.

The sheriff told her it was a Jessie Scout who had attacked her. Similar clues, but what? Similar men? One and the same? It was like trying to untangle a snarled ball of yarn. As hard as her memory tugged at the coiled lengths of skeins, she just couldn't unravel them.

When she arrived back in Washington and Laura's home, she smiled at the welcome she got from both Laura and her mother, making her feel as if she were the visiting royalty.

"We're just so happy to see you back safe and sound," said Laura, as she hugged Jenny.

"It's my turn now to hug," said Mrs. Martin. "I worried about you, Jenny, as if you were my own daughter."

"Jenny," Laura said, "you've had some visitors call when you were away."

"Who?"

"Remember that crazy Zouave who came to the party and claimed you missed your wedding? His name is Michel Dubonnet. and this time he was wearing the regimental blue. He said he'll be back because he wants to invite you out to dinner, possibly this evening."

"Tonight? How could that be?"

"Don't ask me. I don't know."

"Who else came to see me?"

"Martha."

"I wouldn't have thought she wanted to talk so soon after Todd's death."

"Jenny, do you remember her?"

"Sure, don't forget I'd been with the family for a couple of months. Wonder what she wanted?"

"She said she'd return. Oh yeah, almost forgot - Sheriff MacKenzie stopped by to ask to see you in his office whenever it's convenient."

"Jenny, tell us," said Mrs. Martin, "what's the news in the South, outside of the fact they're winning the war?"

"There are shortages already."

"Like what?" asked Mrs. Martin.

"Something even more crucial than corset stays: shoes. Proof that the blockade is working. My sister feels that as the war drags on, there will be more and more shortages; especially, in food, fresh fruits and fresh vegetables that the South had relied on before as imports from other states."

"There's the doorbell, Jenny. I'll take it."

When Laura ushered Martha into the parlor, Jenny scarcely recognized her. With her shoulders hunched forward, eyes cast down, she walked slightly stooped; a portrait of despair. She blanched when she saw Jenny.

"How can you ever forgive me, Jenny?"

"Martha, what are you talking about? Your husband lost his life."

" If you hadn't come when I called you, you wouldn't have suffered the attack at the hands of that criminal."

"Martha, come - sit down over here." Jenny pulled her to a chair.

"Don't blame yourself, Martha, for what happened to me. Remember, I was there because I chose to be.

"Your grief is greater than mine," Jenny said. "How will you manage?"

"I don't know. The loss of Todd hasn't hit me yet."

"If there's anything I can do, let me know."

"I'm hoping, Jenny, that perhaps you and I can get to the bottom of why Todd was killed and you attacked."

"Martha, do you know how many men were out there that night? Could you see?"

"The moon was out," Martha said, "and I was able to clearly watch you as you left the house. There were three men at the door and later they identified themselves as Sheriff MacKenzie and his two deputies."

"Did you see my assailant?"

"Not at that time because he was hiding behind our oak tree."

"Tell me exactly what I was doing at your place."

"You had been writing a feature story about the problem of deserters and why they desert."

"Let's start at the beginning," Jenny said. "Why did Todd enlist?"

"He was offered a bounty like a lot of men and the only condition was to remain in the army for three months, but Todd wanted to stay in for the duration of the war."

"Having said that, then why did he desert and come home?"

"Todd didn't consider himself a deserter. He had gotten dysentery and he was miserable. He wore a flannel belly band, hoping it would give him some relief. It didn't. Then on top of that, he couldn't get a doctor to help him. He even stopped at a military hospital, but there were so many wounded to be cared for the doctors said they just couldn't take the time to help someone who had dysentery. So he did the next best thing - he came home."

"And that isn't deserting?" asked Jenny. "Walking away from your post?"

"He had to come home," Martha said. "In his present condition, he couldn't fight anyone, let alone the Confederates. He planned to return to the Army as soon as he got well."

"Do you really believe that?"

"Of course. Todd never said anything he didn't mean. He never lied."

"Martha, could you see the attack on me?"

"Yes. Todd was at the window with his gun and we saw this man walk slowly towards you. We couldn't figure out why you were going to be a target. We couldn't see his face because a bandanna covered it. The only thing we noticed was that white handkerchief that drooped over his shoulder. When you dropped to the ground, I heard the shot and Todd slumped over. I realized the guy was shooting at Todd and always intended to kill him."

"Do you know if Todd knew his killer?"

"Not only did he not know his attacker, he also didn't know the other men."

"Why was Todd armed?"

"He thought these men were vigilantes. After Todd was shot, the sheriff called out to me, identifying himself and his two deputies and asked permission to enter our house. You were already lying on the ground, Jenny, unconscious."

"The big question is why was Todd killed."

"Whoever your assailant was," Martha said, "I don't think he seriously wanted to kill you."

"He sure had a funny way of showing that."

"I think he had it in for Todd all the time and was using you as a decoy. He wanted to get rid of Todd. I don't think Todd even knew him, was acquainted with him, but he had clashed with him. Matter of fact, Todd didn't know the sheriff and the deputies and they had never identified themselves when they had first arrived, which was stupid because Todd could easily have killed them. He thought they had come to rob him. That's why Todd was there with his rifle."

"Why do you think Todd was murdered?" Jenny asked.

"He knew something and had told me he had wanted to see you as soon as possible to confide in you and seek your advice as to what to do with the information he now had. But you see, he never got around to it. He thought when you came over to the house that night, he'd be able to talk to you, but there was so much excitement going on, he never had a chance."

"So Todd thought that because of this information, his life was in danger?"

"Yes."

"Martha, do you know why the sheriff was there?"

"Neither Todd nor I could figure that out."

"The Army considered Todd a deserter and the sheriff and his deputies were going to arrest him. They had no intentions of killing Todd; they just wanted to take him into custody."

"But that other man who did the killing, wasn't he in the sheriff's party?"

"No. Todd was killed by someone not part of the sheriff's group. This renegade just turned up. The sheriff told me the guy was a Jessie

Scout and that it wasn't unusual for Scouts, like Jessie Scouts, Sheridan's Scouts, or Blazer Scouts to join a posse looking for deserters or Confederate sympathizers."

"Todd told me all about the Jessie Scouts," Martha said, "how they wear the Confederate uniform so they can infiltrate in and out of rebel lines.   As long as they wear that handkerchief in the North, the Feds won't touch them because they know who they are."

"So what's his connection to Todd?"

Martha paused momentarily. "Todd saw a Jessie Scout, outside of an officer's tent eavesdropping. How long he had been standing there and what he heard, no one knows. Todd watched, unobserved for five minutes or so. Then Todd stepped aside when the Union officer left his tent.

"Todd waited as the Jessie Scout entered the tent and left, clutching in his hands some papers that he must have taken from the officer's desk.   Todd challenged him, 'What are you doing? Where are you taking those papers?'"

"What did the guy say?"

"He didn't. Instead, he socked Todd on the jaw and Todd fell to the ground. The Jessie Scout fled, but Todd had seen his face before the attack on him and probably could have identified him.

"There's something I haven't told you, Jenny."

"What?"

"Before Todd enlisted, he made out his Will, leaving everything to me."

"Tell me about it."

"Then when Todd came home, he said he was going to change his Will."

"What brought that up?"

"It happened that on his way home, Todd had stopped to rest. He was exhausted and worn out and a Methodist minister found him lying on the ground, sleeping. The minister asked him if he needed help. Todd told him of his illness. The minister suggested Todd come home with him, to wash up and get a good night's sleep. The minister said he'd let Todd have one of his horses to ride home."

"Then what happened?" asked Jenny.

"I should also mention that the minister's wife gave Todd some paregoric, which seemed to make him feel a lot better and she prepared a light supper for him.

"When Todd returned home, he wanted to reward the minister, his wife, and their church for the kindness bestowed on him. He planned to rewrite the Will, bequeathing the church our 25 acres of fertile farmland."

"I was very angry about that and let him know how I felt. Sure, he was grateful for the aid he received, but he could repay the act in another way."

"Why were you so angry about such a deal?" asked Jenny.

"We have 25 acres of good farmland and that would leave me with next to nothing if anything were to happen to him."

"Wasn't there any money at all?"

"As farmers, we seldom had cash around or even in the bank."

"Under the circumstances, why would Todd leave the church all of the acres, your only source of income?"

"I told him that at least I could always sell the acreage and get some money for it, but donating everything we have of value to the church would yield me nothing."

"What did he say?"

"He seemed unconcerned, saying, 'God will provide.' I was furious and said some very nasty things to him."

"Couldn't he see the problem?"

"He ignored me. I wonder what he would have done if we had had children - if he would have so readily given everything away."

"When was the new Will rewritten?"

"It never was because he was shot and killed."

"Why did he wait so long before thinking of rewriting it?"

"Despite the paregoric, he still felt pretty weak and didn't want to do anything until he was better."

"I'm surprised Todd would even consider such a move," said Jenny.

"The sheriff said he wants to see me whenever I'm ready and since I was a witness to Todd's murder and your attack he'd like me to run through the whole scene with it for him."

"Martha, do you have a question about that?"

"Not really. I was wondering if I should mention the problem with the Will."

"Why? There isn't any problem now. You got everything; there isn't any relevance to what had happened the night of September 24th. What were you planning to tell the sheriff?"

"Just what I've told you."

"Including this?"

"Why not? It's the truth."

"Yeah, but then it puts you in a different light."

"What do you mean?"

"Because the sheriff would think you planned the murder to prevent Todd from rewriting his Will."

"I can't believe that. How could I do that?"

"Maybe you hired this guy to murder Todd."

"Jenny, who would accept such an idea?"

"Anyone is a suspect, Martha, and if the sheriff is looking around for a suspect, you suddenly become available."

"How could he ever prove I had planned Todd's murder?"

"You'd be surprised."

"What should I do then?"

"Just answer the questions he asks you. Let me know when you're going to see the sheriff and I'll go with you to help you relax."

"Will the sheriff let you come in during the interrogation?"

"I don't know; that's up to him. That has nothing to do with my accompanying you to his office. When would you go?"

"Is tomorrow convenient for you?"

"Sure. I'll see you then. Come to the house here and we'll ride together into town."

"You know, Jenny, ever since Todd's death, my conscience bothers me. I wish I had never argued with him. Those arguments were the last memories I had of him and he had of me."

* * * *

"Martha, would you find it too painful to tell me about the events of September 24th?"

"No, Sheriff."

"I've invited Jennifer to stay here," Sheriff MacKenzie said. "Perhaps she will learn those things she doesn't remember and maybe it will jog her memory for other incidents, or will help her in her search for details.

"Did Todd have any enemies?"

"None that I know of."

"Did you have any disagreements with your husband?" Sheriff MacKenzie asked. "Were there any hard feelings between you on September 24th?"

"We had had dinner at 6:00 and spent most of the time arguing about his enlistment, that if he hadn't enlisted, he wouldn't have become ill with dysentery."

"How long was Jennifer with you until my deputies and I arrived?"

"No more than five minutes. She came at 9:55 p.m. and I recall the pounding on the door began at 10:00 p.m."

"Wasn't that rather unusual for Jennifer to come that late?"

"Not at all, because during the day she was busy chasing another story."

"Did Jennifer know that Todd was home?"

"Yes, I had told her."

"When did you tell her?"

"I told her the very day he arrived."

"Which was?"

"September 22nd."

"But she didn't come over on the day he had returned home, did she?" asked the sheriff.

"That's correct. He had been home for two days before I called on Jenny to invite her to the house."

"Why was that?"

"Todd was just too sick to talk to anyone and asked me to wait till he was feeling better."

"Martha, can you tell me what you witnessed that night?"

"The first thing I noticed was the stalker walk slowly towards Jenny and I couldn't understand why. When I heard one of your deputies shout that Todd had a gun, the stalker raised his rifle and fired, killing Todd instantly," Martha paused, weeping.

"Do you want to rest for a minute?" the sheriff asked. Martha shook her head, wiping her eyes. "I saw the Jessie Scout run over to Jenny, who had dropped to the ground when the shooting started, and he struck her unmercifully. I couldn't understand, Sheriff, why you didn't go after him."

"One of my deputies did pursue him, but he was too quick for us and managed to get away without leaving a trace."

The sheriff looked at Jenny. "Did any of Martha's testimony bring back lost memories?"

Jenny shook her head.

"Well, ladies, if you don't have anything else to add, thanks for dropping by and stay in touch."

"Martha, do you feel better," Jenny asked, "now that that's over with?"

"I don't know. There just seems to be so much uncertainty about so many things. I wonder if the sheriff will ever find the murderer. Jenny, come back to the house. I want to show you the Will."

They had just dismounted when the sheriff, accompanied by a stranger, rode into the yard.

"Martha, do you know this man?" asked the sheriff.

"No, I don't."

"This is the Reverend Elias Peterkin. He's a Methodist minister."

"I still don't know him." Martha glanced at Jenny and shrugged her shoulders.

"The Reverend told me that you have his horse," the sheriff said. "Is that true?"

"How could that be? I've never seen this man before."

"When Todd was on his way back home, he was sleeping on the ground when Reverend Peterkin found him, invited him to his house, and the next morning sent him on his way with one of his own horses. Does that sound familiar?"

"Now it does. Todd told me all about that."

"The minister maintans that Todd was so grateful for the kindnesses extended to him, he said he would bequeath the 25 acres you've got here to the Methodist Church. Do you recall that?"

"Yes."

"The minister would like to know when Todd's estate will be probated. Do you remember the pledge Todd made?"

"Yes, I do, but Todd died before he could make changes in the Will."

"Martha," the sheriff said, "how come you didn't mention this in my office?"

"It didn't have anything to do with the events of September 24th."

"Perhaps you might not think so, but it could."

Martha darted a glance at Jenny, then turned to the minister. "Reverend Peterkin, I'll get your horse for you. I want to thank you for helping my husband when he needed help." She went to the barn.

Jenny's eyes popped when she saw Martha lead a beautiful Arabian stallion over to the minister. What was a poor clergyman doing with an expensive horse like that?

"Your husband promised me he was going to rewrite his Will as soon as he got home," said Reverend Peterkin.

"Yes, Todd told me all about that," said Martha.

"Then why didn't he?" Reverend Peterkin asked.

"Todd was still so unwell that he said he would rewrite the Will when he felt better."

"But he didn't, did he?" asked the minister.

"Reverend, he didn't get a chance because he was shot and killed."

The minister took the reins of his horse and then just sat there without a word.

"Reverend Peterkin," Martha said, "I know how you feel. I can give you only a verbal thank you. We are poor people and just can't make even a minimal donation to your church."

"Madam, weren't you poor when your husband came home, too?"

"Yes, Reverend, we've always been poor, eking out a bare existence."

"Then you tell me how could your husband make such a foolish pledge?"

"He was quite overwhelmed with your kindness and hospitality. He had been so miserable and no one had come forward to give him a hand, that he was moved to say what he did."

Without another word, the minister urged his horse forward and left.

"Martha," the sheriff said, "I think you should return to the office as soon as you can so we can get all this testimony down as a matter of record."

"Is that necessary?"

"Yes, it is. No more surprises, Martha?" asked the sheriff.

"None." Martha turned away to reenter her house.

"Jenny, don't forget to stop in before you leave."

"What are you saying, Sheriff?" asked Jenny.

"The lady knows more than she says."

"Impossible."

"How can you be so definite? Has she confided in you?"

"Sheriff, I can't believe this conversation is taking place."

"Well, it is. It's too bad you can't speak freely about the events that occurred in the house on September 24th."

"I would if I could, but I just don't remember. Sheriff, I must speak up in defense of Martha. She's not hiding anything. She's a very reserved person, just like her husband was."

"Jennifer, there is one thing you can clear up for me: why is a young lady like you roaming all over the countryside at 9:55 at night?"

"That's when I arrived here to talk to Todd."

"And before 9:55, what were you doing?"

"From 8:00 to 9:30 I had an interview."

"Wasn't there any other time that you could do that?"

"No, because the gentleman works during the day."

"Is this privileged information or can you tell me who the subject of your interview was?"

"I can tell you. The interview itself was never published because that night was the night of the attack and my memory, having suffered, I was unaware I had interviewed this party."

"Who was he?"

"Secretary of War, Simon Cameron, I know now."

"How did you find out?"

"My editor told me. Luckily, I had my notes and could write up the interview with Secretary Cameron. It should be in the paper next week."

"I'm surprised you can still get it published. Isn't it kind of stale news?"

"The interview was about censorship and that's never stale."

"By the way, Jennifer, who's the executor of Todd's Will?"

"A bank officer. Martha is very upset about that because she knows the executor gets a certain fee of the estate and the lawyer who probates it will get a certain percentage of the estate."

The sheriff laughed. "And if Martha were the executrix, she'd get the amount paid the bank officer."

"What's so funny, Sheriff? I don't get the point."

"Jennifer, since Martha is the sole heir, she gets everything anyway."

"I know that, but with the bank officer being the executor, Martha will probably have to sell some land to pay him his fee, in addition to the fee she'll have to pay the lawyer."

"I wonder what Todd's thinking was, anyway," the sheriff said.

"Perhaps the fact that Martha doesn't know anything about the procedure."

"So then she'd still have to hire a lawyer to plow through all that legal tangle."

"The one issue that Martha was steaming about was the bequest that Todd had promised," said Jenny.

"About the land being donated to the church?"

"Yes."

"This could easily put her under suspicion."

"In what way, Sheriff?"

"If Todd had changed his Will with the new bequest, Martha could have come under suspicion, planning his murder."

"Not this woman. That would be totally out of character for her," said Jenny.

"I don't know about that. If you're left destitute because of such an action, you might resort to murder."

"How?"

"She could have hired that Jessie Scout to do the job, something like that."

"Fortunately, she didn't have to do that and fortunately, Todd never got around to changing the Will," said Jenny.

"Why would Todd even consider such a bequest? Granted, he was grateful to the minister and wanted to show his appreciation."

"Todd was the kind of man who, when he'd receive any act of kindness, his gratitude was overwhelming. He was ready to give the very shirt off his back."

"What was the reason for Todd's appointing a banker to be executor?"

"Todd believed that women didn't understand the prudent use of money."

The sheriff shook his head. "Still hard to figure out the whys and wherefores of a person's mind. Well, Jennifer, I'll be on my way. If you pick up any information, let me know. In the meantime, take care."

Jenny entered Martha's home.

"Jenny, has the sheriff decided to send me to prison?"

"Of course, not. That's farthest from his thoughts."

"Is there something I should worry about?"

"You don't have to worry about a thing. You're innocent. It's just fortuitous that Todd never got around to changing the Will."

"Why do you say that?"

"It could have created problems."

"For whom?"

"For you. But now you can go along, like you've had before. No one will bother you."

CHAPTER III

September 30, 1861

"Sheriff, did you want to see me?"

"Yes, I did, Jennifer. Just to clear up a couple of points about what occurred the night you were attacked."

"Sheriff, I thought the investigation would be under the jurisdiction of the military because Todd was a deserter."

"Ordinarily, I suppose, but since there's a war on now and the military has other things on its mind, I'm elected. Usually the Provost Marshal gets after the deserters. I'd be in on the case anyway because of the assault on you and whoever attacked you also killed Todd."

"Do you have any idea who that Jessie Scout really was?"

"Most times I usually know who's the odd member of our posse. I don't know where this guy had heard of our expedition to go after Todd and I don't know where he came from."

"I think he knew Todd."

"You feel that way, too? Something happened between those two men. Maybe there's a gambling debt that Todd owed, couldn't cough up the money, time ran out, and he had to pay the piper."

"Sheriff, I hate to shoot down your theory, but Todd wasn't a gambling man."

"Maybe, but when the government hasn't paid you for four months, a man could do anything drastic."

"I don't think Todd would gamble even if the chips were down because his own religious views forbade it."

"What were you doing there anyway, Jennifer? You mentioned you were doing a feature on the family. What kind of a feature?"

"I must have known Todd had deserted and I wanted to find out why one would desert at a time when the North depended and needed every man it could get. I'm only guessing the kind of feature I was going to write."

"Then do you recall why he was a deserter?"

"Perhaps he did, but I don't remember that at all, not a single detail. His wife Martha stopped by before she came to see you and she told me why I was there and why Todd was there. Todd had dysentery; there was no doctor around. He was miserable and felt in no way could he fight the enemy feeling like that. He decided to go home, get well, then return to the battlefield."

"Do you really believe that, Jennifer?"

"Yes, I do. Todd was a religious man, an honest man, and a vow meant a great deal to him."

"How long was he in the Army?"

"He joined up right after Fort Sumter and was at Bull Run. He felt very strongly about the preservation of the Union and his duty to fight for it."

"He had a strange way of showing that," the sheriff said, "if he could so easily walk away from his post. He may be an honest man as you say, but he's also very naive. What would happen to our army if everyone decided to get up and walk out? I don't care what the reason is - how can a nation depend on such an army for its security?"

"Sheriff, I've heard that there are lots of deserters walking the streets of Washington, but you went after Todd. Why did you pick on him?"

"The first part of your statement is purely rumor. No one as yet has proved anything about the hordes of deserters on the loose."

"Then who put you on the track of Todd, Sheriff?"

"Jennifer, as a reporter, you should know that one protects one's sources. That's all classified information." He grinned at her. "For a while there, I thought Todd was one of those guys who enlisted for three months, got a bounty, then deserted, and after awhile reenlisted in another district for three months so as to get another bounty."

"Todd was not like that at all. He was a very sincere man and it was a pity he was murdered."

"Now it's my turn, Jennifer, to ask you how you knew Todd had deserted."

"Martha must have told me. I'm sure she was frightened, but of course, I don't remember those details since they occurred just before the murder."

"You said Todd was an honest man and kind. Did he realize that in time of war, deserters are executed?"

"I can only repeat what Martha told me the other day. He was sick with dysentery and had to get medical treatment. He didn't think of himself as a deserter, only a soldier in search of a doctor."

"Did he try to get to a hospital?"

"Martha told me he went to a military hospital, but since the doctors and other personnel were so busy with the wounded, they didn't consider dysentery as an emergency or life threatening."

"Well, Jennifer, I've interviewed almost everyone who came to the open house and so far everyone has a good strong alibi as to what they were doing between 10:00 and 11:00 on the night of the attack. They can all substantiate their alibis, too."

"Then, that's the end of the trail?"

"Not quite. There are two more people I have yet to question and then I don't know what leads to follow. Play it by ear, I guess. I really thought that your assassin would be at the party, but nothing came of that, unless he was there in disguise. You saw everyone: did you see anyone there you didn't know?"

"Wait a minute - the Zouave. Never knew him or saw him before."

"I heard that line he handed you. Some soldier - he comes carrying a silver walking stick. What's he going to do with a cane on the battlefield?"

"Don't forget the kid gloves," Jenny said. "I wonder if that was part of the regulation uniform." She laughed.

"Whatever happened to him?"

"Who knows? He vanished as mysteriously as he had appeared."

"On the other hand, if you learn anything at all, Jennifer, pick up any tips or clues, drop in and let me know."

"I will, Sheriff. I'm going to try to scrounge around for missing pieces of my memory, the attack on me and Todd's murderer."

"Jennifer, if you're thinking of playing detective by investigating on your own, forget it. Nothing good can come of it and it will merely put you in danger. Besides, that's my job."

Jenny laughed. "Sheriff, you're not worried about my taking over your job, are you?"

"You know what I'm talking about. The guy who murdered Todd is vicious. Look what he did to you, and you were only a bystander."

"Sheriff, before I forget - is Martha fully cleared?"

"Jennifer, she was never accused of anything, let alone indicted."

"Are you planning on questioning her again?"

"Not necessarily. I told her to come to the office so that we can get the details of Todd's relationship with the Reverend Peterkin.

"I've been thinking, Jennifer, that maybe the reason you were attacked was because the assailant might have mistaken you for someone else."

"Could be, but I have no idea. I can't think of any of my friends or acquaintances as having murder in their hearts towards me."

She emerged from the sheriff's office when a priest whisked past her, his cassock billowing in the wind. He gave Jenny a cursory glance. She stood there, stunned. She was positive that was the same priest who visited her in the hospital!

She pursued him, calling, "Father, wait! Father, wait!"
She was sure he heard her, but he ignored her, maintaining his pace.

She ran until she caught up with him. "Father, I'm sorry to bother you."

"Then don't."

She realized that after that run, she probably looked disheveled. She had lost the top button to her blouse somewhere. She looked on the ground, bewildered. The priest had not stopped but continued on his walk.

Holding the blouse closed with her hand, she hustled after him. "Father, wait - please."

She reached him and placed a hand on his shoulder to detain him.

He stopped and looked directly at her. He did have grey eyes.

"Young lady - what is it you want?"

"Father, don't you remember me? I was at the military hospital and you were kind enough to visit me."

"You're mistaking me for an Army chaplain. I don't visit military hospitals."

"You didn't visit me when I was in the hospital?"

"No."

"The priest who did was not wearing a chaplain's uniform, either."

"What did you want with me anyway? Make it quick."

"I wanted to thank you for stopping by."

"I see. You understand I call on so many people I can't possibly remember every face and name. Are you in my parish?"

"No."

He walked away from her without another word.

Maybe she was mistaken after all.

* * * *

"Jenny, Michel Dubonnet is coming up the walk," Laura said. The doorbell rang.

"Bon jour, mademoiselle. Is Mademoiselle Jennifer at home?"

"Won't you come into the parlor and wait?"

"Merci."

"Jenny," Laura said, "this is Michel Dubonnet."

"We met at the party, sir, but you were dressed in the uniform of the Zouave then."

"Oui, mademoiselle, but I left the 11th New York and decided to wear the regimental blue so I could join up with the regular army."

"Oh."

"Are you disappointed?"

"No, of course not."

"I was hoping you'd be free this evening so you could accept my invitation to dinner at the Willard."

"Yes, I am free, and I accept your invitation."

"I'll pick you up at 7:00 o'clock. Give you enough time to get ready?"

"Yes."

"Until then, au revoir."

"Well, Laura, what do you think of that?"

"Should I be suspicious or jealous?"

"It's strange, isn't it, that he suddenly discovered me? When he appeared at the party as a Zouave, he acted as if I were his missing bride."

"Jenny, don't let all that charm he oozes hypnotize you. Now let's talk about what you'll wear tonight."

"I should go home and get a dress."

"Not yet."

"Laura, that reminds me - I'm going to have to return home tomorrow."

"Why? Nobody is evicting you. I like the idea you're here, so why?"

"Why not? You and your mother have been wonderful to me, but it's time for me to return to my own place, time for me to put my life back on track."

"Can we talk about that later?" Laura asked. "I have a beautiful black velvet dress, perfect for your dinner date."

"It's not too bare, is it?"

Laura laughed. "It's single breasted. Tiny pearl buttons run from the high neck to just below the waist. You'll love it when you see it. Better hurry or you won't be ready when Mr. Dubonnet calls!"

Jenny couldn't help but admire the lush dress. The sleeves were tight at the wrist and the neck was encircled with a small turned-down collar. The funnel shaped skirt was trimmed with a grey cording.

Mrs. Martin came into the room. "How does it fit?"

"Like a dream," Jenny said.

"As if it were made for you. You look like a princess," Mrs. Martin said.

"She might look like a princess, but there's a black brougham outside drawn by four horses that just pulled up for the Queen of England. Mr. Dubonnet is at the door."

"You look quite beautiful tonight, mademoiselle," he said, tucking her arm into his. "Shall we go?"

"Goodbye, Laura and Mrs. Martin. See you later."

"Chérie, I apologize for asking you on such short notice but I didn't think I was even going to be in the area."

After the waiter brought their dinners, Jenny asked, "Where did you hear about me, Michel?"

"Everyone has heard about you. Besides, when you write for a newspaper like the *Washington Evening Star*, which has the largest circulation of any newspaper around here, you're not exactly an overnight discovery."

"Really?"

"Your feature articles are very popular, in case you didn't know, and I always wanted to meet you. What better time?"

"Too bad now because I'm not really myself."

"Are you talking about your memory loss?"

"Yes. How did you know that?"

"Just about everybody in town knows what happened to you, chérie. That has nothing to do with your being an attractive woman. It just makes you that much more exciting -a lady with a mysterious past."

"Mysterious, yes. But my mind seems caught in a swirl of names and events and when I try to concentrate and push them to the surface, they don't materialize. They evaporate."

"So - you have no recollection at all, then, of what occurred or who hit you. Is that right?"

"Yes, Michel. What did you do before joining up to fight?"

"I was an actor."

"Whereabouts?"

"I performed in New York. Just finished with a production of *Richard 111* right here in Washington at the Grover Theater."

"I wonder if you knew my aunt."

"I doubt it. You and Laura are the only two people I know in Washington."

"No, I'm not talking about this city. I mean New York. My aunt was an actress in New York."

"What play was she in?"

"My aunt wanted to act so badly but all she got were the cameo parts, the walk-on parts. There was a fellow my aunt became involved with."

"What was his name?"

"Len Castle."

"Did he do Shakespeare?"

"No, I don't think so, but he was in *Uncle Tom's Cabin*."

"I don't know anyone by that name. I appeared in that play, too. But he must have been in another production, perhaps, a later one."

"He was a very unscrupulous character. He swindled my aunt out of hundreds and hundreds of dollars."

"Did the police ever catch him?"

"No." She snapped her fingers. "I thought of something. My aunt had a picture of herself taken with him at Matthew Brady's studio in New York. If I showed the picture to you, do you think you could identify him?"

"That might be difficile...difficult. If I don't know the man, I couldn't identify him at all."

"But if you did recognize him, then maybe the police could catch up with him and my aunt could recover the money she lost."

"Is he in costume for *Uncle Tom's Cabin* in that picture?"

"No. You know, my aunt was really crazy about him and she thought the feeling was mutual."

"When did all this happen?"

"Five years ago."

"Where's your aunt now?"

"She's working with a group of Confederate women who want to take over Mount Vernon."

"Then she's returning home afterwards?"

"She won't be home for quite a while because many of the members of this group have invited her to visit them. I don't expect her back for several weeks."

"Eh bien, ma chére, if I can do anything to help, I'll be more than happy to. I'm going to be away too for a few days."

"Oh."

"Disappointed, ma chére?"

"Yes, in a way."

"Why?"

"We're just getting acquainted."

"I'll be back soon." He patted her hand. "That reminds me. I have a dog and when I go away on a mission, I always have the problem what to do with him. I hate to impose, but could you keep him for me until my return? Do you think that Laura and her mother would mind?"

"No, I don't think so. It would only be temporary anyway, isn't that right?"

"Yes," said Michel.

"The dog will be in the backyard which has a fence around it, and he will be tied to a tree."

"I don't know how long I'll be away, maybe only a few days. But the dog has to have a chance to run. He shouldn't be penned up all the time."

"That's no problem," said Jenny. "If I can't take him out, Laura, I'm sure will."

"The waiters are hovering," said Michel. "I think they want our table and want us to get out. I had hoped that Parlor No. 6 would be free tonight so we could visit here a little longer, but I didn't make a reservation in time and was informed that Secretary Seward had reserved it for his party."

"Ma chére, would you have breakfast with me tomorrow morning here at the Willard?"

"Of course."

"Breakfast is served between 8 and 11. I'll pick you up at 8:00. Did you enjoy your lobster tonight?"

"Yes."

"Not too tough?"

"No."

"If you're through eating, then I think we'll leave."

Jenny suppressed a giggle when she saw the Martins on the porch as they watched the approach of the brougham.

"Well, you're home early," Laura said. "Have a good time?"

"Very much."

"How was the food?" Mrs. Martin asked.

"I thought it was good."

"How did it compare with Chez Martin?" she asked laughingly.

"We had lobster," Jenny said.

"Well, that settles that," Mrs. Martin said, "we don't serve lobster at Chez Martin."

"Michel must be very wealthy to take you to Willard's for dinner and in such style," Laura said.

"That reminds me," Jenny said, "he's taking me to breakfast tomorrow at the Willard."

"I've never eaten there," Laura said, "but their breakfasts are supposed to be nothing short of sensational."

"What does Michel do for a living?" Mrs. Martin asked, "that is, before he went into the army?"

"He was an actor."

"With that French accent?"

"Believe it or not, he plays Shakespeare."

"Really!"

"He was in *Richard III* here in Washington at the Grover Theater."

"I wonder if his money comes from French nobility," Mrs. Martin said.

"I don't know. He told me nothing of his background."

"What are you going to wear tomorrow morning?" Laura asked.

"I think I'll wear the same dress that I did at the party," said Jenny.

"Then after breakfast we're going over to pick up Michel's dog. Michel had asked if I would keep the dog while he's gone for a few days. Will it be all right to put him in the backyard until I return home?"

"Sure why not?"

Jenny said, "I can never thank you enough for taking me in like this. But now I feel like my old self except for some pieces of memory that continue to elude me and I'm going to go home tomorrow after I've come back from breakfast."

"So soon?" Laura asked.

"But why now?" Mrs. Martin asked.

"Eventually, I'm going to have to so I might as well take steps in that direction tomorrow."

"You're sure you feel all right to stay alone?" Mrs. Martin asked.

"Yes, I do. I feel a lot better than that day I was discharged from the hospital."

"You feel strong enough?"

"I'll be all right."

"You don't want me to stay with you?" Laura asked.

"You're a dear, Laura, but I'm positive I'll be O.K.."

At 7:55 the next morning, Laura called up to Jenny. "Your brougham is here, Your Majesty, and so is your escort."

"Laura, you're silly."

"At least you're laughing a lot more," Laura said.

At the Willard, Jenny couldn't believe her eyes when she saw the array of dishes for breakfast: fried oysters, steak and onions, blanc mange, and paté de foie gras.

"Oh, Michel, I can't eat all that, even half of that."

"No one expects you to. Eat what you want," he said.

"My stomach hasn't even awakened yet."

"That's what we French say and we always eat lightly, too, in the morning, like a croissant and a cup of café au lait." A waiter approached.

"What will you order?" asked Michel.

"The paté, I suppose, and coffee."

"When we're through eating, we'll stop at my house. I want you to see the dog."

"What kind of a dog do you have?'

"Don't look so worried, ma chére. He's a Labrador Retriever and quite docile."

"If he's so docile, how could he be a good watch dog?"

"He's an excellent one. He'll bark if a stranger were to appear, any stranger."

"How old is he?"

Michel laughed. "Is that going to make a difference? He's three years old. I got him when he was a pup and am the only master he's ever known."

"O.K.," said Jenny, "but will the dog accept me?"

"I don't see why not. Who wouldn't accept a beautiful woman? We'll spend a little time at my place so the dog feels comfortable with you. Then we'll take the dog over to the Martin house. How does that sound?"

"All right, I guess."

"You guess? You don't know?"

"Michel, I'm a little on edge."

"Are you worried about my dog?"

"He doesn't really know me and...."

"I'll show you. You won't have a thing to worry about. I guarantee that; he's that dependable.

"Even though you're staying with the Martins, I'll feel better if you're guarded and if you want to keep the dog until your aunt returns after I get back, I'll be happy to do that. I worry about you, ma chére, and I wouldn't want anything to happen to you."

"Michel, you're very kind and I can't thank you enough."

"That's all I have to hear, chérie." He reached for her hand and kissed it. "You're through eating? Let's go."

As they approached Michel's home, Jenny restrained herself from laughing out loud. The door of this rough hewn log cabin was flanked by two enormous Doric columns of Plaster of Paris.

"That's my one and only concession to classic Greek," Michel said. "Like it?"

"Of course." What else could she say? It was incongruous.

"Perhaps some day I'll be carrying you over this threshold as my bride," he said, as they entered.

She said nothing, but walked into the parlor. It was overloaded with French Victorian furniture - Louis XV. A settee in cherry wood, upholstered in green moiré, occupied one wall, a matching chair stood nearby.

Two Bergéres were strategically placed opposite one another at the fireplace. The seats, curved backs and arms were adorned with floral tapestry, which always reminded Jenny of needlepoint.

"These are beautiful, Michel. Did you bring them from France?"

"Would you believe they're made in the United States?"

"Really?"

"This Louis XV style is so popular that American furniture factories have had French craftsmen come over to help with the demand."

On the wall in the parlor, were three Currier- Ives prints. But the two photos next to them caught Jenny's eye immediately.

"That's Edwin Booth," she said, pointing to one of the pictures.

"That's right. The one and only. He's dressed there as Richard III. Read the inscription to me," Michel said.

"'To the best Duke of Clarence I've ever played opposite.' I'm impressed," Jenny said, smiling at him.

Michel pointed to the other picture. "Do you know who this is?"

"Cordelia Howard."

"You're right again. It sure is. She was Eva in *Uncle Tom's Cabin* in New York in the production in which I played, too."

Jenny read,'No one can play Simon Legree like you.'

What a wonderful keepsake."

"I'll go get my dog," Michel said. "Be right back."

Seconds later, a black Labrador Retriever bounded into the room, tail wagging and barked when he saw Jenny. She retreated a bit.

"Ma chére, he won't bite you."

"How do you know?"

"I already told him not to."

"And he minds you just like that?"

"Of course," Michel said. "Ma chére, I want you to meet Mon Vieux."

"What a strange name for a dog. What does it mean?"

"I suppose you could say Old - how do you say in English fellow?"

"You mean chap?"

"Very good. That's it. But if you call him Old Chap in English, he won't understand."

"Why?"

"He hasn't learned how to translate yet." Michel laughed. "I think you'll like the security he gives you."

"Michel, how thoughtful of you." Jenny petted the dog and began playing with him. She could see he was a docile animal once she got acquainted with him. As long as he barks when he has to; that's what counts.

Michel looked at his watch. "I think we'll have to go. My captain wants to send me out on a mission as soon as possible. I'll drop you off at the Martins' then go on my way, n'est-ce pas? We'll take the buckboard back instead of the brougham. A lot more convenient with the dog in it."

When they arrived at Laura's home, Michel helped Jenny down. He called to the dog, "Mon Vieux, saute." The dog jumped to the ground.

"I'll take a look at that photo of your aunt and her actor friend when I get back." He gathered Jenny into his arms. "Don't forget me."

Michel waved as he returned to the wagon and urged the horse forward.

"Tell us about your breakfast," Mrs. Martin said.

"Let me get the dog tied up in the back first," Jenny said, "and I'll be right in."

"Anything I can do to help?" Laura asked.

"Not really. I'm just going to tie him to this tree temporarily."

"I'm all ears," Mrs. Martin said, as Jenny reentered the house.

"I can tell you this," Jenny said, "your breakfast of buckwheat pancakes and syrup was the best."

"So what was for breakfast at the Willard?"

"Fried oysters, steak and onions, blanc mange, pate de foie gras."

Both Martins groaned. "How did you manage to eat all that?"

"I didn't. I had the paté. There's a midday meal that's even bigger, another dinner at 5:00, a tea at 7:30, served with enough side dishes to make it a supper, and finally another humongous supper at 9:00."

"And an epidemic of heartburn that follows," said Mrs. Martin.

"You're still planning to leave?" Laura asked.

"Yes, I have to, as much as I've enjoyed my stay. I must pick up the pieces of my life again, tell my editor I'm back on the job once more. That, too, will heal me."

"I'll help you move, Jenny. Why don't you ride your horse and I'll take our buckboard and tote the dog in it."

"How about something to eat?" Mrs. Martin asked. "A little snack? Now, Jenny, your breakfast amounted to nothing. Pâté. Ugh."

"Well..."

"Don't give me that. I've already made some finger sandwiches and you can have some tea before you go. It's all settled, girls."

Jenny beamed at Laura and her mother. How lucky she was to have such caring friends!

"Laura, don't look so gloomy," Jenny said. "I'm not moving thousands of miles away."

"I know, but it was so much fun having you stay with us."

"You'll see me around, often enough to get tired of me."

"Never."

"Should we head for the hills?" Jenny asked.

Mrs. Martin had tears in her eyes when she embraced Jenny. "We're always here, Jenny, for you, whenever you need us."

"Jenny, can you come out in the back? I don't think your dog likes me."

"Mon Vieux, behave yourself," said Jenny. He quieted down immediately.

"Is your dog bilingual?" asked Laura.

"I speak to him in English most of the time and a little French sometimes."

"I think you'll need some French to get him in the buckboard."

"I don't think so. Mon Vieux," she called, clapping her hand on the side of the buckboard. "Up, up." The dog jumped into the wagon.

"Come in the house and we'll visit for awhile. You're not in a hurry, are you?" asked Jenny.

"You're sure you don't want me to stay with you?" Laura asked.

"You're a dear, Laura, but I'm positive I'll be all right."

"You won't be afraid to stay alone in this house? You're quite isolated and far from the city."

"Laura, I'm not in a foreign country; only a few miles outside of Washington. Besides, I have Aunt Irene's gun. Did I ever show you the picture of my aunt with that actor she met in New York?"

"Was your aunt in the theater?"

"Oh yes. My aunt wanted to act in the worst way. While she was learning her art, she did walk-on parts."

"Why did she leave New York?"

"She and her friend had a tiff and Irene decided it was time to come home. That was great for me because then I had a place to live."

Jenny went into the library, opened the drawer to the desk. "I can't believe my aunt is still saving this photo. Here's the picture of that guy."

"Jenny, your aunt was beautiful. Who is he?"

"His name was Len Castle; that is, if that's his real name. He swindled my aunt out of almost every dollar she had."

"How did she ever get mixed up with a guy like that? He looks younger than she."

"He was - ten years younger than my aunt who was 45 at the time."

"They sure look like a romantic couple."

"The great romance was over before it began. Sometimes Irene pretends it never happened.

"So why has she kept the picture?"

"Who knows? Maybe for nostalgia. My aunt was quite glamorous- looking for 45. She was flattered with all the attention he showered on her. She used to tell me she had found her knight in shining armor. He was very chivalrous: took her places, brought things to her, candy, flowers, perfume, as if he were courting her.

"He had given my aunt, among other items, a beautiful diamond bracelet. I remember how thrilled she was until she saw the inscription on the back: 'To A.T. from R.T.'

"She asked him, 'Where did you get this?' and he said, 'My uncle had given it to my aunt on their 25th wedding anniversary.' She told him she couldn't accept it. He urged her to wear it and always got a lot of compliments on it.

"Then a woman by the name of Alice Tiernan placed a personal ad in the *Washington Evening Star* a while back. She claimed she lost a diamond bracelet with the inscription on the back of 'To A.T. from R.T.' and said she would like it back for sentimental reasons, and she would reward anyone who returned it, no questions asked.

"Aunt Irene did return it and as far as she was concerned, that was the end of it until she read in the paper of the untimely death of Alice Tiernan. Her house had been burglarized and she had been murdered. She was sleeping in the bedroom, heard a noise, and got up to investigate. He had a gun and killed her. The beautiful diamond bracelet was part of the loot that had been taken."

"And you still want to stay alone here?" Laura asked.

"That all happened years ago. Besides, I don't have a diamond bracelet, but I do have the dog out there to protect me."

"O.K., I'll take your word for it. I better head home or my mother will wonder what happened to me. See you, Jenny."

It was such a beautiful September day, perfect for a hike with Mon Vieux. Jenny walked into the backyard and untied the dog. After a few minutes, the dog began straining on the leash, so Jenny turned him loose.

She watched him first chase a butterfly, then tear after a rabbit. He ran with abandon, reveling in his freedom.

She loved living in the country. It was so quiet, serene. She was the only person on the road as she watched Mon Vieux disappear from sight. Then she began to call him, "Mon Vieux, Mon Vieux," but to no avail. He didn't return.

What was she thinking? She should never have let him loose. If something happened to the dog, Michel would never forgive her. Why didn't she think? But the sky was so lovely and the day seemed so perfect. Now, she wondered, even if she called him, will he respond and come back to her?

She looked behind her. The house was well out of sight. She had walked much further than she planned. She kept on calling the dog. She was beside herself. If the dog ran away and never returned, whatever could she possibly tell Michel when he came home?

She passed a clump of bushes. There was movement from the underbrush in them. Jenny paused. "Mon Vieux?" There was someone or something in there, hidden from sight. It was enough to make her run towards the house or into the middle of the road for safety.

Not a soul around to come to her aid if she needed it. Why didn't she think before she came this far? She knew how secluded the house and its location could be.

She darted a look at the bushes again, determined not to explore that shrubbery. She moved towards the center of the road and cupped her hands over her mouth, calling, "Mon Vieux, Mon Vieux."

Then without warning, a man emerged from the underbrush, wearing what had once been the regimental blue of the U.S. Army. One trouser leg was torn from his knee down to his ankle, and an arm of his jacket ripped off. The uniform was dirty and so was the man. The soles of his shoes were completely worn through.

Jenny stepped back and away from him.

"Don't be afraid. I'm not going to harm you."

"Who are you? What do you want?"

"I'm hungry - haven't eaten in a couple of days."

"Oh." His eyes bothered her. There was a glaze over them as if they were unseeing.

"Could you - would you help me?"

"Right now I'm trying to find my dog. You haven't seen him, have you?"

"What does he look like?"

"He's a black Labrador Retriever."

"No, sorry. Tell you what: if I help you look for the dog, could you give me something to eat?"

She saw him suddenly blanch. "You're not going to faint on me, are you?"

"No. Do you live far from here?"

"Within walking distance. Mon Vieux, Mon Vieux."

"Is that a secret signal to cry for help?"

"Of course not - that's the dog's name."

"I thought you were calling the police nearby."

"There's no one nearby. Why would I call the police?"

"Because of what I am."

"What are you?"

"I mean how I look."

Just then, streaking down the road came Mon Vieux.

"Mon Vieux, I'm so glad to see you." Jenny hugged him.

"Can we go to your house now and get something to eat?"

"Sure." She didn't feel sure, and wondered how she was going to manage this. She decided she would bring Mon Vieux into the house. She'd feel a lot safer.

When they arrived at her house, he walked confidently, a little too confidently up to the door.

"The door's locked," she said, dangling the key in front of him.

She gave the stranger a towel and washcloth and a bar of soap and while he cleaned up, she prepared the food.

"I apologize I don't have too much here because I haven't had a chance to go shopping."

"Anything will do."

"I can give you some rice, hot buttered biscuits, a salad, and jelly cake."

He couldn't gobble up the food fast enough. "I can't thank you enough, Miss."

"Eat as much as you can. If you'd like to take some provisions with you, I'd be happy to pack some for you."

"Thank you. I do have a ways to go yet."

"Where are you headed?"

"Pennsylvania."

"You are far from home. I don't think those shoes you're wearing will make it."

"I don't know what to do about that."

"Buy yourself a pair. Do you have some money for that?"

"Yes, but where can I buy a pair?"

"In Washington. I can give you a ride into town, if you like."

He looked wary. "I'm afraid if I go into town looking like this, I might be stopped and questioned, then if it's discovered who I really am, I'll be arrested. Do you have any horses?"

"I only have one - mine." She fretted that now he might steal it. Suddenly she was afraid; of what, she wasn't sure.

"If I gave you my size and the money, could you go into town and buy me the shoes?"

She'd like to, but leave him, a stranger in the house by himself? She didn't know this man. Who knows what he's capable of? Stealing, for one thing. Face it, she was afraid to leave him here alone.

She turned her back on him and wrestled with the problem. She didn't know what to do. Could she trust him alone in the house? She doesn't know him and he offered no guarantees.

She whirled around and was startled to find him standing right next to her. She saw him remove a gun from his pocket. Her mind raced. Her heart was thumping so loudly she was sure he heard it. She could never overpower him, even if she wanted to try.

His manner, when she found him, was so casual, certainly not threatening, but now that she saw the gun, everything had changed. He can intimidate her because he has a weapon. Thank goodness, Mon Vieux is in the house.

"Would you please back up a little? Give me some room." She couldn't keep the tremor out of her voice.

He returned to his seat at the table. "You said you had only one horse?"

"Yes," she said, barely above a whisper.

He wanted the horse. What was she going to do? She made up her mind she wouldn't let him take it. Yes, she'd fight for that horse. There were lots of stories circulating about deserters wandering through the countryside, robbing and murdering. He's a deserter, she suspected. Before he deserted, he had been in battle and killed men. Think of it - he's dangerous. The words kept revolving in her mind and she couldn't see beyond them.

"I suppose you think I'm an escaped convict," he yelled at her.

She was relieved to see he had put the gun back in his pocket. "I-I don't know what to think," she said.

"I'm a deserter, a U.S. Army deserter. That's why I'm on the run and that's why I can't go into town to buy shoes."

Jenny listened and said nothing. Truthfully, she was still frightened. She looked at him and where the sleeve had been ripped off, she caught a glimpse of a muscular arm. How easily he could subdue her! Whatever was she going to do? She turned her attention back to him, a nagging uneasiness getting the better of her. She made an effort to concentrate on what he was saying. Could she trust him? He was saying something.

"Do you know why men desert, Miss...uh? I don't know your name."

"You won't, either; nor do I care to know yours. As you were saying..."

"Men desert because they're scared. You think about one thing: your own neck. You can hear all about the glory of war, and read about it, but when you're right there on the battlefield, and those around you are falling like toy soldiers, there's a desperate situation you want to do something about, but all you can think of is your own neck."

"If our army deserts, how is the country supposed to protect itself?"

He leaned forward, both elbows on the table. "What do you know about misery?" His lip curled as he spoke.

Jenny remained silent.

"For God's sakes, answer me." He pounded the table with his fists.

"You seem to have all the answers, sir, so why should I bother to reply?"

"All I know is that a great panic overtook me. I began to tremble and shake. I couldn't control it. I had one desire: to run, to run away as far as possible from the battlefield."

"You know what happens to deserters, if they're caught, don't you?" Jenny asked.

"They can be executed." She saw the angry glint in his eyes.

"Not can, but will," said Jenny. She hoped she sounded more confident than she felt.

"You're not going to turn me in, are you?"

"No."

The doorbell rang and Mon Vieux barked up a storm. "Sh-h, Mon

Vieux, quiet."

"Laura, come in."

"Why is Mon Vieux in the house? I thought you were keeping him outside."

"I'll tell you about that shortly."

"I brought your reticule back. You keep forgetting it and I keep forgetting to give it to you."

"Come iñ, come in, Laura. Wait here a minute."

Jenny went into the kitchen. He wasn't there. She rushed to the back door. It was ajar. He hadn't closed it when he left. Her horse! She grabbed Mon Vieux and took him out to the backyard and tied him to the tree, then she sprinted over to the barn and breathed a sigh of relief. Thank goodness, her horse was still there.

"Jenny, slow down and tell me what's going on around here."

"I had taken Mon Vieux for a walk in the country when a deserter, yes, a Federal deserter, popped out of some bushes."

"What did he want?"

"Food. Apparently, he hadn't eaten for a few days."

"You didn't let him in the house, did you?"

"Yes, I did."

"Jenny, a big mistake." She shook her head. You're all alone out here," said Laura.

"I know. It was dumb, but I felt sorry for him. His uniform was tattered and torn; the soles of his shoes were worn thin."

"So he came back to the house then and you fixed him something to eat?"

"Yes."

"What was all this mad dashing about?"

"He was at the kitchen table when you rang the bell and I wanted to see if he was still here. He left through the back door and when I took Mon Vieux outside, I checked the barn to see if the deserter had stolen my horse. He hadn't."

"Then I suppose the reason Mon Vieux was in the house was to protect you."

"Yes."

"Did anything happen - I mean, violently? Did the deserter threaten you?"

"We just talked. I'm glad he's gone."

"So am I. I really think you need somebody to stay with you."

"No. Besides, the worst is over."

"That's what you think."

CHAPTER IV

October, 1861

It was late when Jenny finally settled down for the night. As she began to doze off, a clink entered her consciousness from somewhere. She awoke and sat up in bed. Had she been dreaming? She pricked up her ears. The silence was undisturbed. Not a sound pierced the air, not even the chirp of a cricket.

She snuggled further down into the covers and closed her eyes. Then she woke with a start, all senses alerted. There was someone walking around outside the house.

She heard him step forward on the gravel, then stop, as if he were listening. Then he would crunch forward with two more steps and again, stop and listen.

She heard a clank, followed by a tinkling, like glass breaking. Jenny got out of bed. She looked out the window but couldn't tell whether an intruder had entered the house or not.

The first image that came to her mind was that of the deserter. How could he! After she had been so kind to him and fed him, and this was the gratitude she got for not turning him in! What a rat! Now he's coming back to steal her horse, she supposed. This time, she promised herself, he's not going to get away so easily.

Throwing on a robe over her pajamas, she lit a peg lamp. Holding it with her left hand, she grabbed Aunt Irene's pistol with her right and tiptoed down the steps.

She thrust her head in the parlor. She heard nothing, saw no movement. He wasn't there. She stopped and listened. Where did the burglar go? Is he hiding somewhere? Had he seen her come down the steps? Had she imagined he entered the house?

But where was he? She had heard a window breaking, she'd swear to that! As if on signal, something fell from the mantel on the fireplace and crashed to the floor.

The library! The door was ajar; she pushed it open further and entered. She stopped momentarily to catch her breath, then groped her way to the desk where she placed her peg lamp in a candle socket. She saw him standing at the fireplace. His hands were on the mantel, his back to her. He whirled around.

It wasn't the deserter after all. Now she was more frightened than before because the man facing her was a stranger.

"Freeze. Put your hands up," Jenny said.

"Relax. What are you so aggravated about?"

"Do as you're told. In case you don't know, this is a loaded gun pointed right at you."

"Take it easy. You're not really going to use that thing, are you? he asked.

"Don't bet on it. Maybe I'll hit you in the knees so you can't run away."

"That would be a lowdown dirty trick."

"Don't you feel guilty?"

"Guilty about what?"

"You broke into my house."

"So? I've done nothing and taken nothing."

"You mean I've interrupted you before you did what you had planned to do."

"I don't know what you're talking about. I want to know what are you going to do with me?"

"I'm going to make a citizen's arrest."

"And pray tell - how do you plan to do that?"

"I have several options open, but I don't think I have to discuss them with you."

"Why not? I should at least be informed about my fate."

He inched closer to the desk, resting one hand on it.

"I'm warning you," she said, "Put your hands up once and for all."

"Is this the first warning or the last warning I'll get?"

"You think I'm kidding, don't you? I'm quite serious."

"You shouldn't be holding a gun. You're much too jumpy. Why don't you give the gun to me and it will be better for both of us."

"Not on your life."

"That's what I'm afraid of - my life."

"So stay right where you are. Don't move."

"Would you mind lowering that gun? Are you going to hold me hostage the rest of the night?"

"I might."

"Where will I sleep? How will I eat?"

"That's not my problem."

"Why don't you pack a picnic lunch as long as we have to stay here and glare at each other? I'll make the drinks."

"Stop it! This is not funny!"

"Even if you wanted to scream for help, no one can hear you this far from town. I'm sure you realize that." He took another step forward.

"If you come any further, I will shoot and I mean it."

"Ooh, are you ever tough! I bet you don't even have bullets in that gun. Let me see what you got." He stretched out his hand.

"Oh no, I'm not going to fall for that line," she said.

"You see, I'm not an armed bandit or robber, so put the gun away. Let's sit down and air our differences like civilized people."

"Never."

"Lower the gun at least. A little more. More," he shouted.

"Don't tell me what to do," she screamed at him, trying to remain calm. "Stay right there or I'll shoot."

"You don't appreciate the kind of intruder I really am."

"Shut up." What was she going to do with him? If he calls her bluff, could she - would she shoot? He hasn't really threatened her. He must be up to no good if he broke into the house.

"I didn't come to hurt you or ransack your house," he said.

"This isn't exactly a tea party."

"I know that. That's why I must ask for a fay-ver, a very small fay-ver." He dragged out each syllable.

"You've got to be kidding. I should do you a favor? Don't come any nearer."

"I want to explain to you that this is an honest break-in."

"Is there any other kind?"

"See? I can't finish what I'm saying because you interrupt me all the time. Didn't your mother teach you any manners?"

"Well, say what you have to say already, and get it over with. Just remember to keep your hands up and keep your distance."

"I came here to make a request. My motives are as pure as the driven snow. Have you ever seen me before? Take a good look."

She scrutinized him.

"Do I look like a thug? A gangster?"

She had to admit to herself no.

Before her stood a tall, lean man wearing glasses, late 30s, clean-shaven, tending to bald, and he walked with a slight limp.

His appearance was nondescript and so were his clothes: black pants, dark green shirt. An inconspicuous man dressed in inconspicuous clothes, almost as if he had made an effort to remain inconspicuous.

"Well - have you ever seen me before?"

"No."

"Good because you won't ever see me again."

She glanced briefly at him. The eyes behind those glasses were watchful.

"Before I bid you a fond farewell, I want to remind you, I came here peaceably. I am unarmed and this is how you receive me?"

"You're outrageous. You break into my house to steal and you stand there and tell me you're a man of peace."

"I came in peace, yes - I did."

"Oh, sure - you came in peace by breaking a window. Why didn't you ring the doorbell?"

"At this hour of the night? I'd frighten you."

"And breaking a window to enter didn't frighten me? What was your request? What do you want exactly?"

"This for one," he said as he grabbed the peg lamp and doused it, plunging the room into darkness. Everything happened so fast Jenny was unprepared and just stood there frozen to the spot. He moved quickly, vaulting over the windowsill. She heard him curse as he hit the ground, then his crunching footsteps on the gravel. A horse whinnied and hoofbeats receded into the night as he made his getaway.

She breathed a sigh of relief because she didn't have to use the gun.

Then she realized the dog hadn't barked. The great watch dog - did the intruder kill it?

She slipped into her coat and walked out to the back.

"Mon Vieux, are you there?" The dog ran to her eagerly, jumping on her, his tail wagging. "Are you O.K., Mon Vieux?" He barked as if he understood, and she petted him.

In the morning, Jenny saddled her horse and rode over to Laura's house. "I knew I should have stayed with you," Laura said. "Did the burglar take anything?"

"I don't think I really gave him much of a chance to do anything. Something strange, though - Mon Vieux never barked. I thought that maybe the intruder had killed him. I went out to check on the dog; he was just as frisky as ever."

"The only reason the dog wouldn't bark would be if the burglar had given him something to eat," said Laura.

"The burglar wouldn't know I had a dog until he came to the house."

"I can think of only one other reason why the dog didn't bark: he knew the intruder."

"Impossible, since Michel told me he trained Mon Vieux and had the dog ever since it was a puppy."

"Did the burglar look familiar to you at all?" asked Laura.

"No."

"I have no answers for the dog's behavior then. Do you think you'll keep the dog?"

"I don't know. Michel said that if I decided to keep him until Aunt Irene returns, that would be O.K.."

"Do you think the thief took anythng of value?" asked Laura.

"Laura, I was so upset and anxious to tell you that I forgot to check to see if he had. I believed he hadn't because I didn't give him a chance. Just before he made his getaway, he had extinguished the peg lamp and the room was dark. Maybe he did steal something."

"Let's go and find out," said Laura.

When they arrived at the house and Laura dismounted, Mon Vieux barked at her and wouldn't stop. Jenny went up to him and petted him and told hm to shush. "You see," Jenny said, "he's a good watch dog. He'll bark at strangers."

In the library, Jenny walked around the room. All the books were in place, and nothing seemed out of order. She circled the room twice.

"Well?" asked Laura.

"So far so good," Jenny said as she approached the desk and stopped. "Wait a minute. Remember when you were here yesterday and I showed you that picture of my aunt with that actor? The photo was in a stand-up frame and I had put it on top of the desk."

"You're sure about that?"

"My memory is still good for what happened yesterday. I recall I started telling you about my aunt and this guy who had swindled her. I wanted to show you the picture. It was inside the desk drawer. After you looked at it and we talked about it, I placed it on top of the desk."

"If the thief took it, why would he?" asked Laura. "Certainly not for a souvenir."

"The picture means nothing to him," said Jenny. "Unless in desperation he grabbed the closest object as he fled."

"Jenny, you should report this to the sheriff."

"He'll probably think I'm a ninny the way I acted."

"You behaved like anyone else would if confronted by a burglar."

"I suppose."

"If anything, most people would probably have fired that gun."

"I was glad I didn't have to."

* * * *

"Jennifer, what a surprise to see you here so soon after our last talk," Sheriff MacKenzie said. "Did you run across some clues?"

"No, Sheriff; I came to report a burglary."

"Where?"

"At my house."

"I thought you were staying with the Martins."

"I was until a couple of days ago. I felt well enough to return home."

"Start from the beginning, Jennifer."

"Actually, there isn't too much to tell. I was sound asleep and heard glass break. I went downstairs to investigate. The burglar was in the library. I don't know what he was looking for."

"Did you get a good look at him so you can describe him?"

"Yes."

"Was he wearing a bandanna over his face?"

"No."

"Go ahead, Jennifer."

"He was tall, slender, wore glasses, kind of bald, clean-shaven, and he limped.

"Do you have any idea how old he was?"

"Maybe late 30s."

"How did you protect yourself?"

"I had my Aunt Irene's gun. The robber was not armed. He kept saying he had not come to harm me or ransack the house."

"So what did he want?"

"I don't know, but he seemed to think his burglarizing my home was a big joke. Even my pointing a gun at him was a joke."

"He was a burglar and he must have been after something. Do you keep large sums of money in the home?"

"No."

"Did he take any silverware?"

"He could have, I suppose. Even if he wanted to, I don't think he had the time because as soon as I heard him I went downstairs immediately. He didn't know where the silverware was, and it would have taken him a few minutes to locate it. I'm sure he didn't take any."

"But you hadn't checked, is that right, Jennifer?"

"Yes, that's correct."

"Did he take anything? Did you find anything missing?"

"He took only a photograph of my Aunt Irene with an actor friend of hers, Len Castle. That was about the only item he could have taken because I faced him and blocked his way to the rest of the house."

"Jennifer, you should get a dog to protect you, as long as you're living alone for awhile."

"Sheriff, I do have a dog, a Labrador Retriever. My friend Michel Dubonnet -"

"Who's that," the sheriff interrupted.

"That was that crazy Zouave at the party. He's now dressed in regimental blue and has joined up with the regular army."

"I want to talk to him."

"He's out of the area, but will be back in a few days."

"Now what about the dog? You said it was there on the night of the burglary."

"That's right and he didn't bark at the intruder."

"That's odd. This is your dog?"

"No, it's Michel's and he let me have it while he's gone. There was no way that the burglar knew I had a dog. Michel told me he had raised the dog since it was a pup."

"Do you think the burglar threw some food at it?"

"I doubt it."

"Strange burglary," the sheriff said. "Wonder if it were a flub."

"A mistake? He was at the wrong house?"

"Since he didn't take anything that most burglars would have taken, maybe he had burgled the wrong house, then didn't realize it until he saw you or until he discovered there was nothing to steal."

"There could be another reason, too," the sheriff said.

"Like what?"

"He was at the right house, but for another reason besides robbery."

"Sheriff, that's frightening."

"I'm not trying to scare you, Jennifer; I'm just trying to think of any reason for the break-in. Was there anything unusual about his speech?"

"What do you mean?"

"There are a lot of foreigners around who have joined up with the Union and their speech might be different."

"Such as?"

"Could be heavily accented, or even slightly accented."

"This guy spoke like an American. Even his grammar was good."

"It's a puzzle."

"Well, Sheriff - are you going to work on this?"

"Let's say we'll keep our eyes open for him now that we have a description."

"If you do catch him, what kind of an offense could you hold him on?"

"Probably breaking and entering."

"Not burglary?"

"He didn't take anything of value except that photo of your aunt you described."

"The photo has a sentimental value only."

"Jennifer, let me make sure I got this straight: did the burglar threaten you with any kind of force?"

"Not at all. He seemed surprised that I stood there with a gun pointed at him."

"Did he make any attempt to rush you and overpower you?"

"No, not a bit. He had told me he hadn't come to ransack the house or harm me."

"Very peculiar, to say the least."

"He seemed reasonable, considerate, and...."

"Careful with that, Jennifer," the sheriff interrupted. "Don't be taken in. Remember, he broke into your house. Discarding the theory that he was burgling the wrong house, let's assume he had entered the right house. Don't be fooled by his manner because just below the surface, I'm sure, was the simmering force of violence. He did a good job keeping that part of his character hidden and under control. Maybe that approach of his is one way he cons his victims into dropping their guard, then overpowers them."

"It's hard for me to believe that."

"You haven't dealt with too many criminals, let alone burglars, Jennifer. Did he carry a gun?"

"No."

"Did you see any evidence of a weapon, like a knife, for instance?"

"No. But if he had a gun or knife, wouldn't he have used it?"

"Not necessarily. He might have had a concealed weapon on him and then waited for the right moment to overpower you."

"Totally unreal."

"Count yourself lucky that you got away unscathed. By the way, have you visited the glazier yet? You got to get that window fixed."

"Yes, I stopped there before I came here. He'll be out in an hour."

"Good. That will give me a chance to look at the broken window."

* * * *

Jenny watched the sheriff as he examined the shards still remaining in the window frame. He freed each piece, pored over it, then laid it to the side.

"Not even a drop of blood on any of these," the sheriff said, shaking his head in amazement. "Too bad because if he had been seriously cut, which would require medical attention, I could alert the doctors in the area. Jennifer, do you have a broom and dustpan?"

"Sheriff, leave it. I'll sweep."

"Jennifer, I want to clean this up before the glazier gets here and it gives me a chance to analyze the pieces on the ground."

He got down on his haunches and scrutinized every fragment.

Jenny waited to hear if he found something.

"Nothing," he said, "not a trace of anything. Not even a thread or scrap from his clothing that might have gotten caught. Let's go into the house and I want you to show me where you were standing when you entered the library and where you found the burglar."

"The burglar stood at the fireplace," Jenny said, "with his hands on the mantel. I wondered why he seemed so surprised to see me."

"Probably because he didn't think anyone was home."

"Where did he ever get that idea?"

"Maybe he cased the place before breaking and entering."

"If he had, I'm sure I would have noticed him. As you can see, Sheriff, it is quite remote out here and a stranger walking up the road would cause consternation."

The sheriff inspected the surface of the fireplace. He pushed the ashes around with his foot, then stooped down to comb and sift through them.

He stood up, looked at Jenny, and shook his head. "Nothing, nothing at all. Besides the limp, were there any other distinguishing marks on him? Did he have a scar on his face?"

"No."

"What about his clothes? What did he wear?"

"Black pants, dark green shirt, and he wore black gloves. I remember that because they made him appear ominous. Do you think he's got a criminal record?"

"I don't know. I don't even know why he bothered to break into the house. Was he wearing any boots, like cavalry boots?"

"No. Do you suppose he was in the service?" asked Jenny.

"I don't know. But any little shred, any chip, any bit of any kind would help give me a lead to follow."

"Sheriff, at first I thought he might have some connection to the Jessie Scout or that he might be the Jessie Scout, but it's not possible."

"Jennifer, anything is possible."

"This man was balding and he had a gimpy leg and limped quite noticeably."

"When he escaped out the window, it was a miracle he didn't cut himself to smithereens with those shards of glass sticking up," the sheriff said. "Did he have trouble with his getaway because of that leg?"

"I couldn't tell whether he did or not because he had doused my peg lamp before he vaulted over the windowsill."

"You'd think that a man with a bum leg would have difficulty doing that, too."

"The room was dark. I didn't see him. I heard him swear when he hit the ground. Perhaps he did hurt himself."

"Well, Jennifer, I'll be going. There's really not too much here for me to go on. These house burglaries are always difficult to solve. Is that your dog barking, I hear?"

"Yes, someone must be coming." She went to the door and opened it. "It's the glazier, Sheriff."

"Before I leave, Jennifer, I want to warn you about something. Don't open the door so quickly until you know who the caller is. Look through the window first to see who's approaching."

"I've never done that before."

"You better start now. You were attacked; who knows if the murderer is still out there after you? Also, maybe this burglar didn't get what he came for and might return. Be cautious, Jennifer. Your life depends on it."

"Makes me feel paranoid."

"Be alert as to what's happening around you or to any changing conditions. Don't forget also that when Michel returns to town, tell him I want to see him."

After the sheriff left, Jenny reviewed the conversation she had with him. One fixation dominated her thinking: to recoup the missing blocks of lost memory. Now everything she experienced she tried to link with a trace, a snippet, even a glimmer from the past. The burglary, a dead end, offering nothing.

Thwarted by her own feeble efforts to learn the truth, she discovered just enough to know she didn't know enough.

The flag in Laura's yard - why did that touch a nerve? Unbeknownst to her, it triggered her possible recall of the incident in the schoolyard, culminating her visit with Char, where she relived the appearance of the Jessie Scout who struck out at the flag.

The uniform of the Jessie Scout, clear in her mind's eye became familiar, plucking a bit of the past from her own locked memory. Although the sheriff had identified her assailant as a Jessie Scout, it wasn't until she visited Char was she able to connect her attacker with the Confederate uniform and the white kerchief deployed on a shoulder. Perhaps a secret door will open wider.

With a little time on her hands she decided to visit Martha, look around, and hope to pick up a clue.

She was surprised not to find Martha home. Jenny walked through the yard and tried to replay the little she knew of what occurred that night. The sheriff said she was standing to the side.

She didn't know exactly how far away from the house that was, so she guessed. The sheriff also said the Jessie Scout had hovered over her and he was on his haunches when he socked her. She tried to assume that position.

Her memory was patchy at best. She fumbled and mentally tried to draw out something, anythng with the fragments she knew of an incomplete picture. But there was no way she could assemble any part of the puzzle.

Approaching hoofbeats interrupted her search. Martha dismounted. "Jenny, what are you doing here?"

"I'm trying to fill in some missing blanks as to what happened that night of September 24th."

"Maybe I can help. When I stood at the window, I saw the murderer leave this tree."

"Was he leaning against the tree?"

"Yes, that's how he kept himself hidden. Then he began to stalk you from here." Martha walked the path the murderer had taken.

"Are you sure?"

"Don't forget, Jenny, we had moonlight that night, so I'm quite positive what I saw."

"Was I lying on the ground?"

"Oh, no. You were standing then."

"What happened next?"

"He came close to you and it looked like he was speaking to you."

"It's no use, Martha, I just can't seem to bring it together. Everything remains beyond recall, hidden, as if in a secret file."

"Jenny, come on up for a cup of tea."

"I will, but I want to take one more look at that tree over there. That's where the murderer stood, you said?"

"Yes, I'll go in and brew the tea."

Jenny walked over to the oak and scrutinized the bark to see if there were even a smidgen of cloth caught when the murderer leaned on the tree. Then she moved slowly to the area where Martha said she saw her. Jenny pushed the gravel around with her foot. There was nothing.

She stooped and scooped up a fistful of gravel to examine. All her sifting and searching netted her nothing.

"Tea's ready," Martha called. "Any luck?"

Jenny shook her head. "Martha, do you recall whether the Jessie

Scout walked with a limp or not?"

"I'm sure he didn't, because if he had I'd remember that right away."

"I just seem to be pounding my head against the wall."

"One of these days, somethng will break," Martha said encouragingly.

"Sometimes I wonder."

* * * *

Mon Vieux barked as soon as Laura pulled into the yard with her buckboard.

Jenny came out to greet her. "With Mon Vieux around, I don't need a doorbell."

"Mon Vieux is getting to know me," said Laura, as she petted the dog. "Come shopping with me, Jenny."

"What are you going to buy?"

"Yarn, for one thng. My mother's knitting me a sweater. I'd also like to go over to Topham's and look at some dresses."

Once in Washington they parked the buckboard and began a walk that stretched the length of Seventh Street.

"We can stop at People's and Beall's, too," said Laura.

"Say, this must be a new shop," Jenny said, pointing to Reynolds' Bootery. "Never saw it here before."

The girls stopped to look in the window.

"Jenny, what are you staring at?"

"Those boots in the corner."

"The tasselled Hessian boots?"

"Yes."

"Jenny," said Laura, disturbed at the change in her friend, "do you feel all right?"

"I don't know. Those boots have triggered something in my past, something horrible." She shuddered, then shivered as a chill traveled over her.

"Is there anything I can do for you?"

"Just stand by in case I need to lean on you."

"I wish I knew what's going on," Laura said, glancing fearfully at Jenny.

"So do I." Seconds later, Jenny shrugged her shoulders as if she were shedding a burden. "Whatever it was, it has escaped me as before. Let's go in the store."

"Good morning, ladies - what can I do for you?"

"Those Hessian boots in the window," Jenny said, "are they an import?"

"Aren't you the famous Jennifer Edwards who writes that column in the *Washington Evening Star*?"

"I don't know how famous I am, but yes, I'm Jennifer Edwards."

"Pleased to meet you. I'm Jack Reynolds, proprietor of this store. I always read your column. You know why I like it?"

"No."

"Because you never distort the issue. You report the truth always. I'm still laughing over all those famous war correspondents who had insisted the North won the Battle of Bull Run. That was one of the best columns you wrote. All those geniuses falling over themselves as they rushed to file a story that was the joke of the year.

"Served them right if they got fired for spreading misinformation just because they couldn't wait till the end of the battle. Everyone in a hurry to outscoop the other guy.

"Now, Miss Edwards, it's a pleasure to be at your service. What can I do for you? You said you were interested in those Hessian boots?"

"Not to buy a pair, but just to ask a couple of questions."

"Fire ahead. What's on your mind?"

"Do you remember any of your customers who bought those boots over the years?"

"Not really. Funny thing about that: lot of people admire the boots through the window, and pass by. Sometimes they'll come in to ask the price and then move on."

"So then you're saying that the number of people who have bought the boots is few and far between."

"That's right. What were you thinking of?"

"Would you know of anyone, who stands out in recent memory who bought a pair? Say, from around the last week of August to September 24?"

"Sometimes I wonder why I bother carrying the item because the sales are small."

"Do you keep records as to what customers bought a pair of the Hessians?"

"Let's see if I can help you," he said, stroking his chin and looking at the ceiling. "I made exactly six sales for the period you ask, but no - I do not keep records of individual sales."

"Do you recall any of the customers who did buy during that period?"

"That I do. I sold a pair to Lawyer Cromwell; one pair to my dentist, Dr. Hollingsworth; a pair to, let's see, Dr. Brownell; one pair to Judge O'Donnell; one pair to my wife's dentist, Dr. Ballard; and the last pair was sold to a gentleman who refused to give his name. Paid in cash, though. That was good enough for me."

"You don't know anything about him at all?"

"That's interesting. I know most of my customers by name, like the five I mentioned, and a lot of them come in frequently to the store if only to shoot the breeze."

"And Customer No. 6?"

"I know nothing about him, where he came from or where he was going, except for one thing: he was a Jessie Scout and told me he always buys the Hessian boots because they wear so well."

"Do you happen to remember what date he was here?"

"Yes, and the reason I do is because this is the first sale I've ever made to a Jessie Scout. He bought the boots on September 23rd. I had just opened the store for the day's business and he entered. Gave me my first sale for the day."

"Do you recall what he looked like?"

"Oh yes. Tall, a nice looking chap. Dark hair, pencil thin moustache, otherwise clean-shaven. The kind of guy the ladies would go for. Very courteous. I remember that, too, because, girls, believe it or not, I get a lot of crude characters who drop into the shop. Riffraff. But, of course, the customers for Hessian boots are cut out of different material. Classier, more refined. Yes sirree, gentlemen, real gentlemen."

"Did this Jessie Scout mention where he was going?"

"He did say he had come from around Virginia. Nothing specific, though. No city or town. I had the feeling he didn't want to chat. He seemed in a hurry, also. Are you going to write a feature on Jessie Scouts?"

"Not quite. Did he walk with a limp, by the way?"

"Let me think for a minute." Mr. Reynolds closed his eyes. "No, I don't believe so. If he had limped, I'm sure I would have noticed that right away and remembered it."

"Well thanks, Mr. Reynolds, for your time and help."

"Anything I can do for you? You girls interested in buying some boots?"

"Not today," Jenny said, laughing.

"Well, Laura, what do you think?"

"Sounds like your man, doesn't it?"

"At least we know he was in the area."

"Yeah, but who knows where he is now?" asked Laura.

"When I looked at those boots in the window, I was on edge, jittery."

"I could see that."

"I had seen a pair of Hessian boots like that somewhere before."

As they left the shop, Jenny once again stood before the display window and stared at the boots. She grabbed Laura's arm.

"Laura," she said excitedly, "it's coming back to me as clear as can be."

"Tell me what you see."

"I see the Jessie Scout hovering over me. I'm on the ground so he must have struck me, but not enough to knock me out. I sit up, try to get my bearings, shake my head, and he's there next to me. He's on his haunches. He had hiked up his trouser legs and I see the boots, the Hessian tasselled boots." Jenny had tears in her eyes.

"Oh, Jenny." Laura hugged her. "Still want to finish shopping or not?"

Jenny nodded.

"Jenny, what made you ask Mr. Reynolds about a limp?"

"You know, I told you that the burglar who broke into my house limped."

"Do you think the Jessie Scout and the burglar are one and the same?"

"No, I don't. They're both very different looking men. You heard Mr. Reynolds describe the Jessie Scout."

"So why did you bring up the question of a limp?"

"I thought maybe there was a distinguishable physical mark I might have missed. Try as I might, I'm just not any closer to identifying the Jessie Scout."

"I think you should see the sheriff before you go home," Laura said.

They stopped to buy Laura's yarn and then on to Beall's and Tophams's to look at a new shipment of clothes for the fall and winter that had arrived.

Before leaving for home, Jenny walked into the *Evening Star* to see her editor. Douglas Wallach couldn't have been more delighted to receive her.

"Feel O.K., Jenny?"

"Sure do - well enough to take up my column again."

"Glad to hear that. Lot of folks have been asking about you. Your desk is waiting for you, Jenny."

Half a dozen reporters surrounded her as she left the editor's office. "Back in the saddle again, eh? We missed you and the paper missed you, Jenny."

Jenny rejoined Laura in the buckboard, a big smile on her face. "Where to now?"

"The sheriff's office," Laura said.

"Do you want to come in with me?" Jenny asked.

"Might as well."

Jenny knocked on the door, then opened it, and stuck her head in the room. "Sheriff, are you busy?"

"Jennifer, come on in. What do you have for me today?"

"Laura and I went shopping and passed by Reynolds' Bootery. There was a pair of tasselled Hessian boots in the window. It triggered a reaction in me and I felt that I had seen those boots somewhere, but couldn't figure out where."

"Then what?"

"Mr. Reynolds told me there had been a Jessie Scout who entered his store September 23rd and bought a pair of Hessian boots."

"Did he give you a description of the guy?"

"He sure did: tall, dark hair, pencil thin moustache, clean-shaven."

"That's it?"

"Yes," Jenny said proudly.

"A description like that is going nowhere."

"What do you mean, Sheriff?"

"I can give you hundreds of men who look like that."

"What did you want?"

"About how old was he? What kind of physique did he have: muscular, anemic, well built, or what? How tall was he -5'10", 6 ft.? Approximately how much did he weigh? Got the idea?"

"But, Sheriff, the point is he was a Jessie Scout."

"I hate to disappoint you, Jennifer, but there's not much to go on and that's the problem with this case: not much to go on."

"The other aspect of this incident is that when I left the shop, I stared at those boots and this time, they jogged my memory, releasing all kinds of images."

"What happened?"

"I saw my attack as clearly as if it were happening right before my eyes."

"Let's hear about it."

"I was on the ground so I must have been struck. The Jessie Scout was hovering over me. He hunkered down as I tried to sit up and I recognized the boots he was wearing: Hessian tasselled. He had pulled up his trousers slightly when he squatted in that position. Then he slugged me. Of course, I don't remember anything after that because I was out completely."

"Well, at least we know now your Jessie Scout wears Hessian boots."

"That should be distinctive."

"It is. Aside from the fact these are pricey boots, he must have money for a purchase like that. But who knows where the guy is right now, this very moment, today? Certainly, he isn't going to hang around here."

"Sheriff, I guess I'll just have to dig a little further."

"Now, Jennifer, remember our last discussion about this?"

"But, Sheriff, you're forgetting that reporters are curious."

"Curiosity killed the cat."

"If I promise to come in and clue you in on anything I find or run across, will you give me the go-ahead?"

"No. I'm not going to give you a license to snoop. Besides, you don't need a guarantee to come in and give me any information about this case. That's your duty as a citizen."

"I thought you'd have a dragnet out to catch the murderer already," Jenny said, grinning.

"You see? You don't understand the first thing about an investigation. With an incomplete description, there's no way we can go out to catch butterflies, let alone a murderer."

"At least I know a little about the attack," Jenny said. "I also remember that as he moved in closer for the second blow, I stretched out my hand to stop him, push him back, hold him off from attacking me and my fingers curled around a button on his jacket for support."

"I still have that button, Jennifer. Keeping it here in the safe for use later on as evidence, if and when we catch him."

"Jennifer, in your memory, when you replayed that scene, did you get a close look at the felon?"

"Not really. Don't forget he had a bandanna covering half his face."

"What about his eyes?"

"The moonlight didn't let me see even what color they were."

"I can understand that."

"But I remember his eyes had such cruelty in them that in this scene, I shrank a little away from him before the final attack."

"Something good did come out of this, Jennifer. You were able to recover a portion of your memory. Don't forget what I said about your taking off on your own to search for evidence."

"Yes, I know."

"Your welfare is at stake; remember that. Your safety must not be compromised. If we ever catch the guy, you might be an important witness at his trial."

"Any other stop you want to make, Jenny, before we head for the hills?" Laura asked.

"Home, James."

"The sheriff is right about urging you not to investigate."

"Well, we'll see."

"Don't do anything foolish, Jenny, that you might regret later."

"You know me, Laura."

"That's it - I do. Jenny, listen to me: a lot of people care for you and wouldn't want anything to happen to you."

"I know. But if somebody knocks on my door with some crucial evidence........."

"Comes the day."

"I'm not going to turn him away."

CHAPTER V

Michel walked into Jenny's house like he owned the place.

"Don't you ring doorbells any more, sir?"

"Not when I know who lives here. You naughty girl - you didn't tell me you moved out of the Martins' house."

"I thought it was time to get my life back on track."

"Does that include me, too?"

"Did you have a successful mission?" she asked, ignoring his question.

"Everything worked like an award-winning script.
Did you miss me, chérie?" He kissed her hand, then wrapped his arms around her.

"Naturally."

"Did Mon Vieux behave when I was gone? Did you behave yourself, too?"

"Michel, my home was burglarized."

"Oh, ma chére, I should have been here to protect you." He hugged her again. "He didn't hurt you, did he?"

"No."

"Chérie, did he force you to do anything you didn't want to?"

"Michel," Jenny began to laugh, "please. I had a gun and it was aimed right at him."

"Then did he go?"

"No. He laughed. He thought it was a joke. Everything with that guy was a big joke."

"Even though you pointed the gun at him?"

"Yes."

"Poor chérie. How terrified you must have been at this menace that had entered your life."

"Yes, I was terrified, but not by him."

"Chérie, what are you saying?"

"I was more frightened that I'd be forced to shoot him."

"But isn't that the reason you held a gun to him?"

"Yes, but I didn't want to kill him."

"I thought that Mon Vieux would have protected you."

"Mon Vieux didn't behave well at all. He didn't even bark when the intruder broke a window and entered the house."

"Mon Dieu! He's all right, though, isn't he?"

"Of course. When Laura came to visit, he barked loud and long at her."

"Why do you think he didn't bark when the burglar trespassed?" Michel asked.

"I don't know."

"Did you feed him?"

"I followed all the directions you gave me. Mon Vieux was fed hours before the arrival of the burglar."

"Hm. This is so unlike Mon Vieux. He barks at strangers, I know that. So finally, what did you do?"

"I went to the sheriff to report the burglary."

"Was he interested?"

"Michel, what kind of a silly question is that? He's the law. He'll try to catch the burglar, if he can."

"Exactement, if he can. Most likely, the burglar isn't even around here any more. I should have been here to stop this robber."

"What would you, could you have done?"

"I'd probably end up shooting him, I suppose."

"Michel, do you carry a gun?"

"No."

"Then how would you fight the burglar?"

"I'm in the army, my love, and have access to guns, if needs be."

"I don't think you could do that."

"Why?"

"Because those guns are only used to fight the rebels."

"Who would know the difference?"

"Michel, you'd get in a lot of trouble and make more problems for yourself than you should."

"I'd do anything to protect you, chérie."

"Michel, do you carry a gun when you go on those intelligence missions?"

"No. It would be too dangerous."

"For you or for the enemy?"

"For me."

"Michel, if you were back in France, could you carry a gun?"

"Mais non. Besides, why would I want to?"

"You know, Michel, I know very little about you, about your life, your personal life in France."

He hugged her. "You're worried that maybe I have a wife in France?"

"Well..."

"Chérie, you're so coy. I'm not married. Does that make you feel better? I've never been married."

"How come?"

"The life of an actor is very precarious, very unstable."

"What kind of plays did you do in France?"

"The French theater has a very rich tradition. I worked with a fine company. We did everything from comedy to tragedy."

"Did you do Shakespeeare?"

"Oui, but in French, of course."

"Michel, did you ever wonder how a French detective would solve this murder case?"

"He would have solved it already. There'd be no question about that."

"Even if he didn't have any evidence?"

"Oui, even if he didn't have any evidence."

"Well, Sheriff MacKenzie is working hard but hasn't as yet latched on to any hard evidence that will give him a good lead. Speaking about the sheriff, I have a message for you: he wants to see you."

"Have I done something I shouldn't? Do you know, ma chére, what does he want?"

"The sheriff has been talking to everyone who showed up at the open house. The sheriff had seen you there and asked me if I knew you. At the time I didn't."

"But then we became better acquainted, n'est-ce pas? We'll have to make up for lost time."

"Never mind about that, Michel."

"When the sheriff inquired again, you told him?"

"Is that all right, Michel?"

"But of course, I understand. Will you do something for me?"

"What?"

"When I go to see him, will you come with me?"

"I don't know if the sheriff will permit that."

"I need some moral support, chérie." He reached for her hand and brought it to his lips. "Just holding your hand like this will give me courage."

"Of course I'll go, if you want me to be there."

"Does the sheriff know anything about me?"

"Not that I know of."

"Have you told him about our relationship?"

"No, did you want me to?"

"Not particularly. I'm sure it will come out during his questioning."

"I wouldn't worry about it, Michel. You've done nothing, committed no crime."

"You've made me feel better already. Let's get back to the burglary. Did you recognize your burglar? Did he look familiar at all to you?"

"I never saw him in my entire life."

"If I had been here, I would have saved you."

"Thank you, Michel. You're sweet."

"Thank goodness, you had Mon Vieux, n'est-ce pas?"

"No, it isn't so, Michel. Mon Vieux never barked to warn me, I told you. How could that be?"

"C'est formidable. I don't know. He should have barked at an intruder. Did you check him out after the burglar fled?"

"That's exactly what I did and he seemed as frisky as ever."

"What means 'frisky'?"

"Lively."

"I'll have to look into this. Ma chére, did the burglar take anything?"

"Yes, he took that photo of my aunt with Len Castle."

"You mean the picture you were going to show me to see if I could identify that guy? Quel dommage! That's too bad. Come with me - I want to go out in the yard and see Mon Vieux for myself." He linked his arm through Jenny's as they left the house.

"Mon Vieux, Mon Vieux," called Michel. The dog ran to him, wagged his tail, and jumped on him. Michel petted him and scratched him behind the ears.

"Mon Vieux, why didn't you protect Jenny? Pourquoi? Why? He certainly looks and acts normal to me."

"Maybe he was sleeping," said Jenny, "when the burglar broke into the house."

"He would have awakened if he heard a noise, like glass breaking."

"Who wouldn't awaken to that?" said Jenny.

"I don't understand."

"Neither do I," said Jenny.

"Chérie, has the sheriff been here to investigate?"

"Yes."

"Only yes? Did he find anything?"

"No."

"What did he look at?"

"The broken glass."

"Where the burglar had entered the house?"

"Yes."

"What did he find?"

"Broken glass."

"No blood where the burglar might have cut himself?"

"Nothing, Michel, absolutely nothing."

"Did the sheriff come into the house, too?"

"Yes, in the library."

"He found no trace of anything?"

"There was nothing to find."

"Chérie, you should be careful wherever you are and wherever you go. Do you check to see the doors and windows are locked before you retire?"

"Yes, I've always done that."

"There's a lot of lawlessness around."

"What do you mean?"

"Deserters, stragglers, fugitives."

"Oh."

"These are desperate men and who knows what they'll do? Are you in frequent contact with the sheriff?"

"I'm sure he has been hearing too frequently from me with one thing after another."

"You're entitled."

"But, Michel, there are other people here who live on the outskirts of Washington who also depend on him and his services. Speaking of the sheriff, Michel - how would you like to see him today and get it over with?"

"I don't like the way you said that."

"Why?"

"You make it sound like an ordeal."

"Michel, you're so theatrical!"

"Come with me, chérie. Hold my hand."

"A big strong man like you has to have his hand held? I don't know. Depends on the sheriff - he might not like another person in the room during the interrogation."

"If this is going to be an inquisition, I could use some moral support."

"Why? You haven't done anything."

"What did the sheriff ask you when you first saw him?"

"At that time he was concerned about who had attacked me. He wanted to know if I had any enemies."

"That's laughable. How could a beautiful girl like you have enemies?"

"He thought my assailant might have held a grudge against me."

"Against you? Impossible!"

"Angered about something I wrote. Who knows?"

"Chérie, how should I act when we go to the sheriff?"

"Natural."

"You mean without clothes?"

"No, no," Jenny said, laughing. "Just be yourself."

"What if the sheriff asks me a question I don't like, do I have to answer or can I ignore it?"

"No, no, Michel, you must answer all questions."

"And if I don't?"

"You'll only antagonize the sheriff and I don't think you'd want to do that."

"Non, non."

When they entered the sheriff's office, Jenny asked, "Would it be all right if I sit here during the interrogation?"

"As long as Mr. Dubonnet doesn't object."

"Mais non, of course," Michel replied.

"Your full name?" Sheriff MacKenzie asked.

"Michel Dubonnet."

"Are you an American?"

"I am français."

"Why did you come to the United States?"

"I came to help fight the rebels like Lafayette came to help fight the British."

"In what branch of the service did you enlist?"

"The Union Army. Je ne comprends pas. I don't understand the question."

"Do you know your regiment? Brigade? Your superior officer?"

"No, because I do not exactly fight. I'm on intelligence missions only for General McDowell."

"Before you joined the army, what kind of work did you do?"

"I was an actor."

"Here in the United States?"

"Oui."

"What was the last play you were in?"

"*Richard III.*"

"Have you known Jennifer for a long time?"

"No, but every day we get more and more acquainted, n'est-ce pas, chérie?" He looked at her and grinned.

"Has Jennifer told you that she has been struck on the head by an unknown assailant and that she has had a temporary loss of memory?"

"Ah, oui. It is such a pity - a beautiful girl without a memory."

"Mr. Dubonnet, where were you on the night of September 24 between 10:00 and 11:00 o'clock?"

"I was in a play."

"Where?"

"Grover's Theater here in Washington."

"The play?"

"*Richard III.*"

"What role did you have?"

"The Duke of Clarence."

"Approximately, how long was the performance of the play?" Sheriff MacKenzie asked.

"About 2 1/2 hours, I think."

"Since the curtain went up at 8:00 o'clock," the sheriff said, "then it was over at 10:30. Does that sound right?"

"I guess so."

"So between 10:30 and 10:45 what were you doing?"

"Taking curtain calls."

"Can you support that alibi?"

"M'sieu," Michel began to laugh, "I have the whole audience in the theater to testify in my behalf."

"But *Richard III* is no longer playing in Washington," Sheriff MacKenzie said. "It would be rather difficult for me to find out who was in the audience that night."

"Oui, after the production finished here, the company went on to New York."

"Who can vouch for you?"

"Members of the cast and especially, Monsieur Edwin Booth who played Richard III."

"Why didn't you go to New York with the rest of the company?"

"I decided to stay in D.C. and join the Union Army because I wanted to do my share in saving this country from breaking apart."

"Allowing time for curtain calls - you said 10:30 to 10:45," the sheriff continued, "I think we're talking about 11:00 to 11:15 and even 11:30 until everyone, including the cast, left the theater. Is that correct?"

"I don't know."

"Where did you go afterwards?"

"The Willard Hotel."

"Why? What was going on there?"

"Since this was our last production of *Richard III* in this city, we had a cast party."

"About what time was that?"

"Je ne sais pas. I don't know. Close to midnight, maybe 11:45. I don't know."

"Can you pin it down a little more?"

"I don't remember."

"Do you recall how long you stayed at the party?"

"Till one or 2 A.M., I think. Closer to 3 a.m."

"Can't you be more specific?"

"Sorry. Can't"

"In what parlor was the party held?"

"I don't know."

"Was it Parlor #6?"

"The champagne was flowing and we were all doing our share of drinking. I just don't remember."

"Is there anybody at the party who can verify your story?"

"Probably Edwin Booth."

"He's in New York now, isn't he?"

"But he would have remembered I was there. He was the least inebriated."

"You're very vague about when you left the party, Mr. Dubonnet. Do you have any idea about what time, more or less, it might have been?"

"Sorry. I just don't recall. I guess I was really out. Later I was told that it was Edwin Booth who called a cab and took me home and put me to bed."

"I'll have to get a list of the cast from you because I'll have to check on your alibi and get some of these times more accurately."

The sheriff then became suddenly grim. "After this war, Mr. Dubonnet, what are your plans?"

"Moi? I will return to la belle France, of course. Sheriff, why are you asking me all these questions?"

"Because everyone is a suspect until I catch the murderer. Everyone will be questioned. I have to know where you were on September 24th between 10:00 and 11:00 and what you were doing. Every moment has to be accounted for."

The sheriff rose, extended his hand to Michel. "Thank you for stopping by. Will you be in the area for awhile?"

"Well, M'sieu, it all depends on what mission I'm sent to perform."

"I understand. Goodbye, sir."

"Au revoir, Monsieur."

"Now was that so bad?" Jenny asked, as they walked over to Michel's buckboard.

"I suppose it could have been worse," Michel said. "I'll take you home, Jenny."

"Jennifer!"

"The sheriff's calling you," Michel said.

"May I see you for a minute, Jennifer?" The sheriff beckoned with his finger.

"Chérie, I will wait for you."

"How are things going?" Jenny asked.

"They aren't - I can't seem to scratch the surface of this case yet.

I just want to ask you a few questions. I don't make a connection of that Jessie Scout to anyone else. Maybe all the hunches I've had are wrong, too. I had hoped to prove my theory right.

"What else did Mr. Reynolds have to say about this guy's description?"

"That he was the kind of man the ladies would go for."

"That's a big help! Ladies' man, sure - also a murderer. Does that count?"

"Doesn't look too good, does it?" asked Jenny.

"There isn't a shred of anything I can get my teeth into. All your guests with their credible alibis - all verified. No one has a remotest connection with anyone else, except for the fact most of your guests were journalists."

"Then do you believe Michel's story?"

"I have no other choice for the moment, that is, until I hear from Edwin Booth."

"Where do we go from here, Sheriff?"

"Frankly, I don't know. Do you know who Joe Barton is, Jennifer?"

"Isn't he the maitre d' at the Willard?"

"Yes, he verified the cast party in Parlor #6. That would be September 24th. He had attended a performance of *Richard III* on September 23rd, and commented on Edwin Booth's acting as well as that of Michel Dubonnet's as outstanding. Both very fine actors."

"I wouldn't expect any other comment."

"Have you seen the play?" asked the sheriff.

"No, but I've seen enough evidence such as photos in Michel's home autographed by Edwin Booth, lavishing praise on Michel for his role as the Duke of Clarence."

"Jennifer, will you forgive me if I ask you a personal question?"

"What is it?"

"How serious are you about Michel?"

"You don't pull any punches, do you, Sheriff?"

"No sense in hemming and hawing. So, can you answer that?"

"I've made a point of keeping my relationship with Michel light - playful, if you prefer, nothing else. Up to now, he has done nothing to indicate he's serious about us as a couple and that's fine with me."

"Do you know anything about his background? Is he married? Does he have a family?"

"He already told me he has never been married."

"Did he tell you why?"

"Yes. He said that the life of an actor is too unstable and uncertain for family life."

"What about his own family - his parents, his siblings?"

"He has never said anything. Perhaps he has none."

"Do you know the source of his income?"

"Outside of his acting career and now he's in the Army, I have no idea. Why do you ask, Sheriff?"

"For a guy who's an actor and now in intelligence work, he sure throws the money around."

"I'm surprised you even mentioned this."

"Jennifer, in case you didn't know, when you arrived with Michel at the Willard in a four horse drawn brougham, a lot of people took note. Where does he get the kind of money for that and to dine at the Willard on the salary of an actor or on the pay of a soldier? Can't be."

"I don't know and have never asked, of course."

"I wonder if he comes from French nobility."

"I don't know, have no idea. I can tell you he has impeccable manners."

"I have to figure out who had the motive, the means, and the opportunity. Was Todd's murder premeditated?"

"I think you've already established that, Sheriff."

"That's about all I know at this date. Don't forget - if you pick up any information, I expect you to tell me."

"I will."

"What did the sheriff want?" Michel asked when Jenny rejoined him in the buckboard.

"If I said nothing, would you believe me?"

"No, I wouldn't."

"Well, it's the truth. He told me he's quite baffled about the fact the case is going in circles as nothing has happened."

"Do you expect me to believe that for all the time passed in his office that's all he had to say?"

"Michel - I'm surprised at you!"

"I have a very obsessive curiosity when it comes to you or anything about you."

"Well, you can relax. That's all that was said. Really, nothing of any consequence."

"I find it rather strange," Michel said, "that the sheriff would call you into his office and admit to you that he has no leads and doesn't know how to pursue further and solve a murder case."

"Michel, you have a suspicious mind."

"Maybe, but why would he tell you these things?"

"Sheriff MacKenzie and I are friends, good friends and -"

"Are you and he lovers?"

"Michel, please! He's old enough to be my father!"

"That means nothing. Sometimes a man who wields a lot of power has a lot of sex appeal for a woman."

"Stop!" The tears rolled down Jenny's cheeks.

"Why are you crying?"

"Because I'm laughing so hard. Since we are friends, the sheriff is concerned about my memory loss and the fact I was attacked."

"I believe you, chérie."

"I should hope so."

"Will you be home tomorrow?" Michel asked.

"I expect to."

"May I call on you, mademoiselle?"

Jenny giggled. "Michel, you're so so silly. You can call on me on one condition."

"I know: that I ring the doorbell. Until tomorrow, chérie."

As soon as the doorbell rang, Mon Vieux barked up a storm in the yard. Jenny glanced out the window before opening the door to Bert.

"What a surprise! What are you doing here?" Jenny asked.

"I've been to see the sheriff and thought that was an excuse enough to come to see you," said Bert.

"So tell me - what did the sheriff ask you?"

"He wanted to know if you and I are lovers."

"I don't believe you. The sheriff is looking for answers to the crime."

"As I was saying," Bert explained, "it's a crime that you're not giving me the kind of attention you're lavishing on Michel."

"What else happened at the sheriff's?"

"You wanted to know what the sheriff asked me and I told you. I told him that we hadn't arrived at a relationship yet where we could be called lovers, but it will be soon. Is that O.K.?"

"Forget about that and you can wipe that stupid grin off your face while you're at it. Now give it to me straight: what important questions did the sheriff ask? What else did he want to know?"

"He asked me if I knew Michel. I said I knew of him and could recognize him and I said that was easy because Michel was always seen in the presence of a beautiful woman."

"Bert, do me a favor and get Michel out of your system."

"That's a prescription for you."

"What did the sheriff want to know?"

"He asked me where I was on the night of September 24th between 10:00 and 11:00 o'clock and that was all."

"And how did you answer that question?"

"What question? Oh, about my whereabouts on September 24th? That's all privileged information and I can't disclose that."

"Do you have a good tight alibi?"

"I think so."

"Did anybody ever tell you that you can be a pain in the neck, Bert?"

"I was practically told that on July 21st at the Battle of Bull Run."

"I'm trying to put together pieces of my memeory that elude me as to what happened that night when I was attacked and how it came about and you're about as much help as General McDowell fighting the rebels."

"I told you everything! I don't know what you want!"

"You know damn well what I want. Where were you on the night of September 24th between 10:00 and 11:00?"

"You don't think for a moment that I was the guy who hit you, do you?"

"If I don't get any answers, what could I possibly conclude except that you're hiding something? Your reluctance to tell me based on what you call confidentiality won't work because if the culprit is found and the case goes to court, all of this and more will become part of the testimony and the public record."

Bert stroked his chin. "I thought the sheriff's interrogation was to be kept secret."

"Oh, for heavens' sakes, Bert - do you think if I learn something I'd be shouting it from the roof tops?"

"All right, all right. Let's see, now, what was I doing on the night of September 24th...um...."

"Yeah, sure, tell me about the alibi you got and make it good."

"I don't know how to start."

"From the beginning."

"Well, it's like this -"

"Cut the baloney already."

"I'm trying to."

"You're the most exasperating male I've ever met," said Jenny.

"You mean next to Michel?"

"I'm waiting."

"I was invited, along with war correspondents Carmichael of the *Philadelphia Enquirer*, Harry Hoffman of the *New York Herald*, to Secretary Cameron's farm in Harrisburg, Pennsylvania for a couple of days, September 23rd and September 24th."

"Why couldn't you have said that in the first place? Why the runaround?"

"It's probably the same kind of line Michel hands you these days."

"How do you know?"

"I won't go into that."

"Anything important discussed at Secretary Cameron's?" Jenny asked.

"Censorship, for one. It's the age old question: how much should the public know? We journalists believe that we have a duty to keep the public informed, you know that."

"Did Secretary Cameron have a solution to the problem?"

"He made a lot of statements to placate us, but he emphasized that as long as we don't reveal any news of camps, troops, military and naval movements except by permission of the general in command, we can write our dispatches."

"So what's left to report? You know as well as I, Bert, that a general - any general - isn't going to allow us to release the kind of information you mentioned, or even the kind of information we want to print."

"The point is," Bert added, "that if you were to write a feature about some aspect of the war, you'd eventually bring in snatches about military movements, troops, camps, and so on to give your story a bit of authenticity."

"What bothers me even more," said Jenny, "who's going to anoint himself as the censor to decide what the public should or should not read?"

"Secretary Cameron put a little teeth into that when he reminded us that he had Lincoln's approval to invoke the 57th Article of War, providing the death penalty for giving information about the army without the sanction of the commanding General."

"These guys always like to tie the hands of the press," Jenny said.

"But that's not going to stop someone like Carmichael. Carmie told me he's going to really dig for confidential informatin when he's after a story, and he doesn't care whom he steps on."

"I wouldn't want the reputation he has," said Jenny, "especially if he thinks he can pull some underhanded trick to get a scoop. His notoriety will make any story with his byline suspect."

"Maybe. But Carmie really knew how to butter up Secretary Cameron. He talked and wrote about Cameron as if he were the Messiah. Secretary Cameron wrote a letter to Chief Censor H.E. Thayer telling him not to suppress or change the wording of any telegram that Carmie sends. Can you beat that? I'll tell you - the guy's a real operator."

"But what about us?" Jenny asked. "Don't we have that right to enjoy the same privileges, too?"

"That's a moot question."

"There's something else that Secretary Cameron is overlooking," she said, "the families of the men on the firing line. Aren't they entitled to know about their sons, brothers, husbands?"

"The issue gets stickier and stickier."

"Remember what happened this past April when the Sixth Massachusetts arrived in D.C. from Baltimore?"

"I wasn't there," said Bert.

"Too bad - you missed a great story. I was there at the station when the train pulled in."

"I heard about the ruckus through the grapevine. It must have been frustrating."

"Most of us felt the families should know what was going on. Wouldn't you, if you had a brother in the Sixth and it was stoned by a secessionist mob? There were a lot of casualties."

"I recall Carmie telling me when you reporters got the story from the men and dashed over to the telegraph office at the Willard, a squad of National Rifles blocked the entrance. No messages could be sent."

"I didn't have to send my story over the wire because I worked for the *Evening Star* then, but my editor said the story could not be printed by orders of Colonel Charles P. Stone."

"Yeah, well, I was interviewing the Secretary of State in his home," Bert said, "when members of the press pushed themselves right into the parlor where we were sitting, and boy, did they make the noise about the edict! Secretary Seward claimed he didn't know who was behind the order, but he said he thought it would be better for morale to keep the lid on the Baltimore story."

"I hope we don't have to go through something like that again," Jenny said.

"Before I forget - Jenny, how would you like to meet General Sherman?"

"Where?"

"I have secured all the necessary papers and some passes to get us by train to Muldraugh's Hill, Kentucky."

"Then when we get there, what happens next?"

"We'll talk to the General about getting a pass from him that will let us move easily and freely in and out of Union lines."

"Sounds good. When do we leave?"

"I have to get one more pass that will permit us to leave Washington and then we'll be off. By the way, the sheriff asked me about the burglary when I saw him," Bert said.

"Did he think you had done it?"

"Of course not." He glared at her. "Can you tell me about it?"

"I was asleep and the burglar broke a window. I had my aunt's gun and I confronted him."

"What did he say?"

"Nothing. He thought his break-in was a joke."

"Did he take anything?"

"Just a photo of my aunt with an old boy friend."

"Strange. How did he get away?"

"He extinguished the light I had and vaulted over the window-sill."

"Didn't the dog bark to warn you?"

"No, and no one has answers to that. The sheriff has been out to see if he could scare up some clues."

"Did he find anything?"

"Outside of the broken window, there was nothing."

"Jenny, listen to me. That guy might return."

"Maybe. Who knows? I have Mon Vieux to protect me."

"The dog isn't worth anything."

"He barked when you came here."

"But the important thing is he didn't bark when the burglar broke in the house, so what kind of protection is that?"

"What are you trying to say, Bert?"

"I'll stay here tonight."

"Uh, uh. That's out."

"Don't worry. Your virtue won't be compromised."

"It's not necessary for you to stay."

"I'll sleep on the couch in the parlor."

"Why are you so insistent that the burglar will be back? Why would he even risk a chance of getting caught? A second time? Unbelievable."

"It's quite apparent he didn't get what he wanted."

"How would you know?"

"Come off it, Jenny. The guy breaks into a house and swipes a photo? If this were a Rembrandt, I could understand. But a photograph?"

"I suppose you're right." She paused. "Unfortunately. Well, the least I can do is offer you supper."

"Fine. I'd like that."

"I hope you don't mind leftovers."

"Is that what you serve Michel when he comes here?"

"Do you want to leave now? Right now?" She stood with her hands on her hips and stared him down. "If I hear one more word out of you about Michel, you can walk."

"Look, I'm sorry about that. I'm just worried about you and Michel."

"You can stop right there. You're just like yesterday's headlines."

"What do you mean?"

"Dull, stale, flat."

"Say it. Dead."

"Touché."

"So what's on the menu?"

"Come into the kitchen and you'll see for yourself."

"These are leftovers? They look good enough to eat."

"They are."

"Can we eat now?"

"Sure, why not? Let me tell you first what you're eating so you won't accuse me of poisoning you. Leftover chicken, leftover cranberry sauce, leftover sweet potatoes, and leftover pumpkin pie. Everything has been reheated. Almost forgot. Fresh salad of romaine and lettuce and tomatoes."

"This is good food," Bert said, nibbling on a drumstick.

"You mean for 'leftovers'?"

"Tastes fresh to me."

After dinner, Jenny cleaned up the kitchen and Bert went into the parlor with the evening paper.

"Do you have a gun, Bert?"

"No."

"How do you expect to protect me?"

"I can fight with my fists."

"Against a gun? He probably has a gun."

"Did he use it with you?"

"No, but that doesn't mean he wasn't carrying one."

"If I hear him," Bert said, "I can surprise him by overpowering him."

"I'm going upstairs to get some sheets and a blanket for you," Jenny said. She couldn't have been gone for more than a few seconds when she heard Bert snoring already. He had slumped into a pillow, his feet on the couch, fast asleep.

Some guard he is. "Bert, wake up." He didn't respond. She slapped him gently. He opened his eyes, slightly disoriented.

"Where am I? Oh, Jenny. Too heavy a meal."

"You can't sleep on my aunt's couch. For heavens' sakes - it's an antique. There's a sofa at the other end of the room. That's for you."

"Hm," was the sleepy reply.

"Bert, get off the couch. Now."

Still no answer. She'd settle this once and for all.
She removed his shoes, then grabbed both legs, pulling him off the couch. He landed with a thud on the floor, none too gently.

"What in blazes. - ?"

"You'll have to sleep on that sofa over there. This is an antique; you can't sleep on it."

"It looks like a daybed to me."

"Oh please, deliver me! Get off that couch! Move! Now pay attention. We have to put one sheet down first on the sofa. You do that. That's the sheet for you to lie on and then you can cover yourself with this other sheet and this blanket."

"Why are you talking to me like I'm a 6 year old? I'm here to protect you. Who knows what that guy will do?"

"Yeah, sure."

After the bed linen had been spread and Bert crawled into the covers, he said, "Aren't you going to kiss me goodnight?"

"Nope. I'm going to check to make sure the doors and windows are locked. Goodnight."

Jenny dozed off quickly. A few hours later she heard Mon Vieux bark. She sat up and listened. He continued to bark.

She scrambled out of bed, grabbed her robe and Aunt Irene's gun. How had the intruder managed to enter the house despite Mon Vieux's barking? She didn't hear any glass breaking. Did someone actually break into the house? The dog continued to bark. Of course, the "great guardian" isn't awake yet.

Jenny ran down the steps, but halfway, she caught her foot on her nightgown and hurtled over the remaining stairs, stopping her free fall by clasping hold of the newel post.

"Bert, are you up?" A snore answered the question. This calls for some ingenuity, she thought. She stood at the bottom of the steps and belted out a bloodcurdling scream.

First, a groan emanated from the parlor, then Bert woke up. "What the hell's the matter with you?"

"Didn't you hear Mon Vieux?"

"So what? Is that what you awakened me to hear? Go away; I want to sleep."

"Bert, there must be somebody walking around outside the house. Mon Vieux wouldn't have barked otherwise."

"Don't bet on it. If that dopey dog didn't bark when there was a break-in, what makes you think he's going to bark when there isn't a break-in?"

"I think there's a trespasser outside."

"Now that you mentioned it, I'm sure I saw someone wearing a cap."

"A kepi?"

"Could be."

"Union or Confederate?"

"Do you realize you woke me from a deep sleep?"

"Then how could you have seen a guy wearing a kepi?"

"I didn't. Must have been dreaming. I was so groggy and disoriented, I didn't know what was going on."

"Then why did you bother to sleep here if you're so put out because your sleep was disturbed?"

"In case you forgot, I was staying here to protect you."

"Glad you told me - I wouldn't have known!"

"If you had been here alone, would you still have screamed?" Bert asked.

"What would be the point of that? No one would have heard me. Sh-h - listen."

"What?"

"Mon Vieux stopped barking. Maybe he was barking at an animal?"

"You mean like a tiger?"

"No, silly, a rabbit or -"

"Or what?"

"Maybe he was having nightmares."

"Now I've heard everything. You've had the dog for a couple of days or so and all of a sudden, you're an expert on canine care." He stood up, stretched, and walked towards the door.

"Where are you going?"

"Home."

"Aren't you going to stay for the rest of the night and protect me?"

"With a scream like that you can scare anybody away." You don't need protection. I'll be back in a couple of hours or so with a cab to pick you up to go to General Sherman's."

CHAPTER VI

"Before we get moving," Bert said, "you should know that when we arrive at General Sherman's let me do the talking."

"Why?"

"I've seem the General before and I'm hoping that his acquaintance with me will make it easier for us to get the pass we need."

"So you want me to stand there like a dummy?"

"That's the idea."

"Well, that's not my idea!"

"Hey, Jenny, this news story is for both of us, so why the complaint? Besides, if you start talking, you might give the General the wrong signals."

"Oh, is that right!"

"Jenny, I'm doing you a big favor by taking you."

"Gee, thanks."

"Look, if you don't like the arrangement, forget about it. Stay home."

"You'd like that, wouldn't you?"

"Don't be ridiculous. I offered to take you so you could get a good story, a real story."

"What's that supposed to mean?"

"Let's face it. How much longer can you keep your readers on the edge of their seats with tales about the shortage of corset stays?"

"Coming from a guy who thought the North won the Battle of Bull Run, that's quite a compliment."

"Should we stop snapping at each other and declare a truce?" Bert asked.

"The column just wasn't about corset stays. It was about the effects of the blockade on the South."

He chuckled. "Sorry about that. You see, I didn't get past the corset stays to find out what the rest of the column reported."

She restrained the urge to slap him.

"Before you start screaming at me, you might think about the Federals and Confederates wounded and dying on the battlefield and the least of their worries would be about the shortage of corset stays."

"You bastard!"

Jenny looked forward to a pleasant train ride. Instead, she sat with her back to Bert, gazed out the window, seethed, and refused to speak to him the entire journey.

Big deal, Bert thought. She's giving me the silent treatment. Let her stew. Who cares? Once we get our story about Sherman, she'll thank me for it.

"It's difficult to please you," Bert said.

"Then try harder."

General Sherman was at the railroad station at Muldraugh's Hill when they arrived.

Bert greeted him. "General, how are you?" He extended his hand, but Sherman ignored him.

"General, let me introduce myself."

"Don't bother."

"I'm Bert Wells from the *New York Herald*."

"Sir - you're wasting my time," General Sherman said.

"We've met before, remember?"

"I'm trying to forget it."

"And this is Jennifer Edwards of the *Washington Evening Star.* I'd like you to inspect the letters of introduction and passes that I brought with me."

"You keep them," was the surly reply. "I'm not interested." Turning to Jennifer, General Sherman said, "So you're the young lady who wrote that feature about absenteeism."

"Yes, sir."

"Let's see - you described it as one of the most serious evils facing our military."

"General, I'm flattered that you should remember my very words."

"Flattered? You should be arrested and shot as a spy."

"General, I don't understand."

"Well, maybe you'll understand that reports like that about hundreds of officers - you did say hundreds, didn't you?"

"Yes, sir," Jennifer said meekly.

"And thousands of men are almost continually away from their command posts and that many of them are deserters and stragglers. This newspaper story is giving information to the enemy and they must have been jubilant to know we had a vast army that is at all times AWOL."

"I don't know what to say, General. I-I didn't think."

"That's the trouble with most of you newspaper people - you don't think what impact your writing will have. And now you come to me to ask for a pass so you can infiltrate the lines. In no way will I have irresponsible reports going out to newspapers, giving the enemy advance hints of our plans and problems."

"General, I'm under a lot of pressure," Bert spoke up, "from my editor to get the story."

"There is no story here," the General said. "Get that through your head once and for all."

"I'm only after the truth, General," Bert said.

"We don't want the truth told about things here," General Sherman said. "That's what we don't want. Truth, eh? You miss the point. No, sir, we don't want the enemy any better informed than he is."

The General stopped to look at his watch. "It's 11:00 o'clock. The next train for Louisville leaves at half past one. Take that train. Be sure you take it. Don't let me see you around here after it's gone."

"I was hoping, General, you'd give me a pass so I could move freely in and out of the lines."

"Give you a pass? Hah! Sir, you have exactly two hours to get out of this place or I'll hang you both as spies."

"All I'm asking for is a pass," Bert persisted.

"General," Jenny interrupted, "if you don't want to give us both the pass, then just give it to Bert."

"No passes. There will be no passes," the General shouted. "How many times do I have to repeat myself? I can't make that any stronger. I have steadily refused to admit reporters of any kind within my lines. You people make the best paid spies that money can buy. Jeff Davis owes more to you correspondents than to his victorious army."

"General, I want to remind you," Bert said, " we came all the way from Washington to interview you. My readers are hungry for news. They want to know what you're like, how you think, everything about you."

"Even my favorite color?" the General asked dryly, arching an eyebrow in Bert's direction.

"You're a hero, General," Bert said.

"You want news? Stay in Washington. That's where the news is. You've come to the wrong place for news. The subject is closed. I've made my decision."

Bert continued. "You won't consider the pass, sir? It would mean a lot to us."

"I'm sure it would. We don't need newspaper people moving through the lines wreaking havoc with their rhetoric."

"Then, I guess I'll have to do the best I can," Bert said.

"If that means you're going to follow through with your plan without my pass, let me warn you. If I find either or both of you moving among the lines, I'll arrest you and hang you both as spies."

"Without due process?" Bert asked.

"Since when are you a legal expert? The Constitution does not guarantee the right to report. The First Amendment protects only the right to print."

"I know that," Bert said.

"I consider the press alone responsible," the General continued, "for all the defeats so far of the Federal armies and that includes Bull Run. If I had my way, I would pay the government to buy up all the printing presses in the country at the price of diamonds and destroy them. I'm warning you for the last time: you better be on that 1:30 train or else."

There wasn't much to do after that except to wait for the next train and return to Washington.

"I thought you said Sherman had met you, Bert, and had an acquaintanceship with you," Jenny said.

"He did."

"Well, he must have amnesia because he didn't exactly welcome you like a long lost son."

"As far as Sherman is concerned, it's open season on reporters."

"Wasn't your friend Carmichael behind that story accusing Sherman of being insane?"

"Well, that was a misunderstanding."

"Misunderstanding, nothing! Carmichael got the recognition and the notoriety he wanted."

"A slight exaggeration."

"Not at all. Every paper in the country carried the story. It spread like wildfire. No wonder Sherman is sour on correspondents."

"I don't think Carmie really meant what he wrote."

"If he didn't mean what he wrote, then why did he write it? Look at the reception we got. We had barely stepped from the train and Sherman presented us with an ultimatum: get out or else."

"Well...."

"One thing about a hotshot journalist like Carmichael and his mission in life to dig for the scoop of the century. He screws it up for the rest of us when we try to plumb the same source for a story. He forgets that we all have to make a living at this game."

"You see how irascible Sherman is," Bert said.

"That's his personality, but that doesn't mean he's insane."

"I think the reason Carmie said that was because of Sherman's attitude toward reporters."

"Still, that doesn't excuse headlines claiming Sherman was off his rocker."

"I still think that when Sherman told Secretary Cameron he needed 200,000 men, that set everyone off."

"Since he was the General, wouldn't he know if his forces were deficient and how many men he needed?"

"Carmie told me," Bert said, "he thought it was a sign of panic."

"I can't believe that generals become panicky. I'm surprised you even came to see the General. Certainly you must have known how he felt about news people," Jenny said, her voice rising in anger. "With Sherman's reputation, being what it is, it would be impossible to persuade him to budge and give you a pass."

"What's eating you?" Bert asked.

"I'm annoyed because this was a wild goose chase and I could have stayed in D.C. and worked up another feature of my own. The day was a total loss."

"Hardly. Can you think of a better way for me to woo you from that Frenchman and have you all to myself?"

"Grow up, Bert."

Once they arrived in Washington, Bert hailed a hack and took Jenny home.

"Would you like to go out to dinner tonight?" Bert asked.

"I'm quite tired. I'll pass, but thanks anyway."

"Look, Jenny, I'm sorry the way things have worked out today."

"I know you did your best. That's the way it goes. Truthfully, I can see General Sherman's point of view. Oh, here we are."

"There's a man at your door," Bert said.

"That's Michel. Wonder what he wants. Come on over; I'll introduce you."

"Do I have to?"

"Stop being such a prig. Michel, " she called and waved. He walked towards them. She saw the bouquet of roses in his right hand.

"Why don't you take these?" Michel said, handing her the flowers. "After all, they're for you."

She saw Bert roll his eyes heavenward. Nuts to him. "My favorites," she said, plunging her nose into the bouquet. "How did you ever guess?

"Michel, I'd like you to meet Bert Wells of the *New York Herald*. Bert, Michel Dubonnet."

"How do you do?" they both said simultaneously, two heads nodding in unison. Like wind-up dolls, Jenny thought. They didn't shake hands. Jenny was convulsed with laughter. They were both so grim sizing up each other.

"Well, I'll be talking to you, Jenny," Bert said. "Nice to have met you, Mr. Dubonnet."

"Same here."

Thank goodness for convention, Jenny thought, otherwise they'd probably whip out sabers and duel. She watched the waiting cab move away and tried hard not to grin.

"Why are you smiling?" Michel asked.

"Something struck me as funny."

"Share it with me?"

"It's just silliness. Michel, would you like to stay here for dinner tonight?"

"Yes, that would be nice, but aren't you tired?"

"Not really. Do you like oysters, Michel?"

"My favorite."

"I've got the next best thing to it: mock oysters."

"Why are they called 'mock'?"

"Because they're really a fake."

"I do not understand."

"What would you call then oysters made from a mixture of corn, eggs, butter, flour, and fried in oil?"

"Not oysters." He laughed.

"My sister gave me her recipe. With the blockade tightening like a noose around the South, it's more and more difficult to get products and so she has to use Yankee ingenuity even if she lives in the South."

"Your sister is a Confederate?"

"Not really. She's married to a Southerner."

"He's in the war, I suppose," said Michel.

"Yes - that's why she wants to stay where she is."

"What does she do?"

"She used to teach school, but now the school's closed."

"Where is it?"

"What I call just over the border, this side of Centreville in Virginia."

"Is that schoolhouse," Michel paused, thinking, "in a cul-de-sac?"

"Yes - how did you know?"

"I do a lot of intelligence gathering for the Union and I passed it one time and thought the building was abandoned."

"How long ago was that?"

"Maybe a month or so."

"What made you think the schoolhouse was abandoned?"

"There were no children present and then there was that flag." He paused, as if picking and choosing his words.

"What about the flag?"

"It was flying high on a flagpole, but in streamers as if someone had slashed it with an axe. The whole place was forlorn, depressing. If there were somebody there, that flag would have been replaced, I'm sure."

She wanted to ask him if he had been there that day she had seen the Jessie Scout hack away at the flag, but she didn't.

"Michel, I've often wondered when you go on these missions, are you dressed as a Federal or a Confederate?"

"I don't wear the Union uniform because I'd quickly be captured and probably hanged as a spy."

"Oh, Michel. So what do you do?"

He laughed. "Are you trying to pry out all my secrets, chérie?"

Jenny felt her face grow warm. "No."

"Not even for a feature for your column?"

"I wouldn't take advantage or cash in on any information you'd give me from your private life."

He was still chuckling. "I know that, chérie. Let's go back to how I dress for my secret....You know they're secret, don't you?"

"Yes."

"Missions. I have to keep my identity as a Federal hidden always so sometimes I'll wear a Confederate uniform."

"And the other times?" she asked.

He grinned. "You don't miss a beat, do you? Other times, I'll dress like a sutler and come with pies and cakes, the kind of food the Southern soldier likes. You'd be surprised how much information I can gather in that role. Now, does that answer all your questions?"

Jenny nodded.

"Should we start with some sherry?" Jenny asked. "Trés bien." He raised his glass to Jenny's. "To you and success. What kind of success would you like, Jenny?"

"I'd like to find the man who killed Todd on September 24th."

"Why is that more important to you than a personal success?"

"Because if I can achieve that, I'll know who battered me."

"Chérie, I cringe every time you speak of this."

"Wouldn't that be uppermost in your mind if you had been attacked by a murderer?"

"I suppose it would. I never gave it any thought. Is Sheriff MacKenzie still working on the case?"

"Yes, he is."

"Is he getting any closer to solving the crime?"

"I don't know since he doesn't discuss the daily progress with me."

"Well, let's get back to you. How was your day?" Michel asked.

"I suppose it could have been better. Bert Wells had arranged for us to interview General Sherman."

"You went all the way to Kentucky?"

"Yes. Anyway, the General was supposed to give us a pass so we could move freely within the lines."

"What happened?"

"Nothing. General Sherman despises all correspondents and he made a point of letting us know at once."

"So you didn't get a story?"

"That's right. We boarded a train for home."

"I have a little gift for you, Jenny, that will make you feel better about your rotten day." He pressed a small box in her hand.

"Can I open it now?"

"Absolument."

Inside the satin lined box on a cushion of black velvet, rested the most exquisite diamond bracelet Jenny had ever seen. She smiled at Michel. "It's beautiful, just beautiful."

"I'm glad you're pleased. It is a stunning piece of jewelry, isn't it? Let me put it on your wrist, Jenny. There."

"Michel, thank you. I don't know what to say."

"Then why say anything?" He wrapped his arms around her and kissed her. "Now, isn't that a better way to say thank you?"

She moved her arm away and scrutinized the bracelet. "Elegant, really elegant."

"That was a wonderful dinner, Jenny. I'll always remember the 'lock'."

Jenny interrupted, laughing, "Mock, Michel."

"Oysters," he said.

"I'm glad you enjoyed them. If someone really likes oysters, this recipe might be hard to take."

"Not at all," he said, squeezing her hand. "Jenny, remember what I told Sheriff MacKenzie that I was going to return to France after the war?"

"Yes."

"Would you come with me?"

"Oh, I don't know. This is kind of sudden."

"Why is it so sudden? I just gave you a diamond bracelet. Doesn't that mean anything?"

"Yes, but the United States is my country...."

"And La Belle France is mine. Is that why you can't come with me?"

"I'd have to think about it."

"Would you have to spend less time thinking about it if I asked you to marry me?"

"I'd have to think about that, too."

"Eh bien, we have time. The war won't be over for quite a while, a long while. Afterwards, we'll see. In the meantime, we can be together, can't we, chérie?"

"Of course, Michel."

"Since the interview with General Sherman was an aborted one, suppose I told you," Michel said, "I can do one better than your Mr. Wells."

"Michel, he's not my Mr. Wells. He's just a professional colleague."

"Whatever. Do you want to hear my proposal or not?"

"Yes."

"How would you like an interview, a real interview with General Beauregard?"

"You're not kidding?"

"No."

"If you only knew what that would mean to me!"

He smiled. "Suppose you ask the General what turned the tide for him at Manassas."

"Do you think he'd talk about that?"

"Why not? The battle was fought three months ago. It's history now."

"Would that be a scoop for me!"

"I know the General and he won't disappoint. Besides, he owes me a favor, a big favor."

"Where's the General today?"

"At the moment, he's in the area, but I don't know how much longer that will be. Eh bien - can you go tomorrow?"

"Even if I couldn't, I would."

"I knew you wanted this and while you've been gone, I spoke to the General and he said he'd be happy to receive you."

She threw her arms around Michel and hugged him.
"Michel, I'm so excited over such a story and that you made all this possible."

"Chérie, I've been thinking of you a lot the past few days. That's why I wanted you to have the bracelet. How have you been feeling lately?"

"Much, much better."

"Do you feel well enough to do the interview?"

"This interview? Oh yes."

"And your memory - has it improved?"

"There are still too many loose threads I simply can't weave together."

"So how will you regain your memory?"

"The doctor said it would take time and I must not force, and be patient. Perhaps in a month or two. It seems like eons ago since I was attacked."

"Now that I'm here," Michel said, "I won't let anything like that happen to you again, ever." Michel frowned, then said, "What surprises me is that Sheriff MacKenzie was there when you were attacked, but he didn't do anything to rescue you."

"Everything happened at once, that's what I was told," said Jenny. "Todd, the deserter, appeared at the window with a gun, and the assailant fired at him, killing him instantly. Then I was on the side, and before the assailant made his getaway, he came over to clobber me. The sheriff told me he ordered one of his deputies to pursue, but the assailant was just too swift."

"So to this day, the sheriff doesn't have any idea as to the identity of the assailant. Is that right?"

"Yes. Let's talk about something else."

"It's not pleasant for you, n'est-ce pas?"

"No."

"Until tomorrow, then, ma chére."

A few minutes after Michel left, Jenny got ready to go. She could hardly wait to show Laura. The bracelet gleamed on her wrist like a crown jewel. She opened the door to find Bert standing there.

"I didn't get a chance to ring the doorbell," he said. "Were you expecting me?"

"No. I'm getting ready to leave the house."

"Then I came just in time, didn't I? Here," he said, thrusting a bouquet of flowers at her.

"What are these for?"

"How come you never questioned Michel when he gave you a bouquet?"

Jenny looked at the bedraggled weeds in her hand.

"What are these?"

"Wildflowers."

"Where did you get them? Along the side of the road?"

"Is that important? What do I have to do to please you?"

"When you do something, do it with style."

"By style, you mean like dinner at the Willard Hotel? A bouquet of a dozen roses? I can't afford that on my salary."

"Then don't bring me anything."

"You don't say that to Michel."

"Stop competing with Michel. Just be yourself without the fanfare."

"I thought we could spend some time together today."

"Not today. I'm in a hurry to go."

"Got a late breaking story?"

"If I did, I wouldn't tell a competitor."

Bert watched her as she mounted her horse, waved goodbye to him and galloped away. Where could she go in such haste and why? To see Michel again? He followed her at a respectable distance. He watched her as she stopped at Laura's, dismounted, and entered the house. So this was where the big rush ended up?

Bert rode back to Jenny's, removed the bouquet he had brought that Jenny had discarded on the porch, and threw it in a nearby field.

* * * *

"Jenny, anything wrong? Feel all right?" Laura asked, greeting her at the door.

"Nothing is wrong and I feel fine. I want to show you the gift Michel gave me," she said excitedly, as she extended her wrist.

"Oh, what a beauty! Let me call my mother to see."

"Call your mother to see what?" Mrs. Martin asked as she entered the room. Jenny thrust her wrist forward.

"Magnificent," Mrs. Martin said. "Where did you get it?"

"Michel gave it to me."

"Oh."

"He wants me to marry him."

"Oh."

"He wants me to return to France with him."

"How do you feel about that?" Mrs. Martin asked.

"I told him I have to think about that."

"Think about it for a long time, Jenny - I don't have to tell you that a person's life can be reduced to nothing, destroyed by one moment's wrong decision. Without sounding dramatic, Jenny - this is such a moment."

"Jenny, could you take the bracelet off your wrist so I can examine it closer?" Laura asked.

"Sure."

Laura automatically flipped the bracelet over. "Jenny, have you seen this?" The inscription on the underside read: "To A.T. from R.T."

The girls looked at one another.

"I never bothered to inspect it," Jenny admitted, "but then again it never occurred to me and why would it? Michel clasped it on my wrist and I've worn it ever since."

"What are you thinking?" Laura asked.

"I don't know what to think, but I'm sure there's a logical reason for that."

"Do you know where Michel bought it?"

"No. That would be the last question to enter my head when someone gives me a gift."

"Why is that inscription so important" asked Mrs. Martin, "even though you're not A.T.?"

"My aunt, five years ago, had been an actress in New York."

"I didn't know that," Mrs. Martin said. "Irene is keeping secrets from me."

"She became involved with an actor by the name of Len Castle," Jenny said. "Aunt Irene was crazy about him. He plied her with all kinds of gifts. Then he gave her a diamond bracelet."

"Like this one?" Mrs. Martin asked.

"I can't believe this is the same," Jenny said. "I'll say almost identical, even though it has the identical inscription on it."

"Then what happened?" Mrs. Martin asked.

"I should mention that Len Castle swindled my aunt out of hundreds of dollars."

"If he didn't have the money," Mrs. Martin said, "I wonder where he got the money to buy the bracelet."

"Maybe he didn't have the money," Jenny said. "He was a con artist; he could have stolen it. I don't know."

"Continue," said Mrs. Martin. "What happened to Irene's bracelet?"

"My aunt returned to Washington and found a personal ad in the *Evening Star*. The ad was placed by one Alice Tiernan who inquired about a bracelet like this and she disclosed the inscription on it. She stated that if it were returned to her, there'd be a reward and no questions asked."

"Did Irene track her down to verify if she were the real owner?"

"No, Aunt Irene didn't because she felt the fact that since the lady mentioned the inscription - no one else would know about that except the owner herself - that she was speaking the truth."

"So what did Irene do?"

"She returned the bracelet. Then some days later we read in the paper that Alice Tiernan had been murdered by an intruder who ransacked her house and stole the bracelet."

"Sounds suspicious," Mrs. Martin said. "I always thought there was something shady about Michel, didn't you?"

"You mean you think Michel is behind this?" asked Jenny.

"Don't you?" asked Mrs. Martin.

"Not at all. Are you saying he murdered Alice Tiernan?"

"I won't go that far," said Mrs. Martin. "Still, the circumstances surrounding the bracelet are strange, you'll have to admit that. Don't you agree, Jenny?'

"I don't know what to think. I do know that he has always been a gentleman in the true sense of the word. A charmer, yes, but a gentleman always."

"Don't fall for that," Mrs. Martin said.

"I'm sure there's a logical explanation as to how Michel acquired the bracelet."

"It will have to be mighty logical to convince me," Mrs. Martin said.

"Well, I'm too poor to be swindled," said Jenny, "if you think he's a con artist."

"I wouldn't put anything past him. The next time he kisses your hand, count your fingers afterwards."

"Mother!" Laura yelled.

"I accept his feelings towards me as sincere," said Jenny.

"Be careful, Jenny, just be careful."

"Why do you feel like that?" Jenny asked.

"Call it intuition. Can't put my finger on it, but there's something about him I find disturbing."

"Well, I have no complaints. He has been considerate and very kind."

"Jenny, remember I once told you you're like family? Now I'm telling you don't do anything you'll regret."

"If you mean like marrying him - that's the farthest from my thoughts. I wouldn't give up my career for anyone."

"Did Irene finally get over her great love?"

"She did, but it was a very painful experience for her."

"And what about the police? Have they ever caught up with this Len Castle?"

"Never. He disappeared. Who knows where he is? Today Irene couldn't care less."

Bert was waiting for her when she returned.

"Don't tell me you've been here all this time?"

"Just about. Can I come in? I have something important to tell you."

"You're so serious!"

"Does the name Phillip Sorenson ring a bell?" Bert asked.

"Phillip Sorenson. I know a few people by the name of Phillip, but no one with the surname Sorenson. I give up -Who is he? Why should I know him? Not another war correspondent, I hope."

"Nothing like that. Private Phillip Sorenson is in the Union Army. He's in artillery. Does that help stir the memory?"

"Bert, the name means nothing to me. Stop with the games. Who is he? Where have you been? How did you meet him and why?"

"One question at a time," Bert said, enjoying her bewilderment. "First, I went to see your friend Martha."

"Why?"

"From Martha, I got the story of how Todd had seen the Jessie Scout rifle some papers from the tent of a Union officer and -"

"I know all about that," Jenny interrupted.

"But you didn't share it with me."

"Go on," said Jenny.

"Then Martha told me that Todd had confronted the Jessie Scout as he exited from the tent and the guy cuffed him, knocking Todd to the ground."

"I know all that, too."

"Well, I figured somone else had seen the attack on Todd."

"So what did you want from Martha?"

"I wanted to find out the company number, regiment, brigade, whatever. Martha had kept all of Todd's letters and that information was on the return address of the envelope."

"Bert, that was a wonderful idea!"

"You finally appreciate me for a change. Should I continue?"

"There's more?" she asked eagerly.

"Oh yes," he said, delighted he had her full undivided attention.

"How did you ever get there?" Jenny asked. "I mean - into the encampment."

"I got a pass from General McClellan."

"As easy as that?"

"Once I told him what I was trying to find out, he actually became sympathetic."

"Then what? And where was the army?"

"The army was encamped near Leesburg, Virginia. It looks like there might be a battle shaping up soon in that area, too."

"Get back to your story."

"I had less trouble than I thought I would locating Private Phillip Sorenson. Sorenson told me he saw the Jessie Scout strike Todd. The next thing Sorenson knew was the Jessie Scout asked him to help move Todd's body to another area, away from the officer's tent."

"Then, afterwards, did you get around to talk to Sorenson, inteview him?"

"Yes."

"Did Sorenson tell you why the Jessie Scout had hit Todd?"

"Yes, the Jessie Scout said that Todd had owed him some money."

"Did Sorenson give you a description of the Jessie Scout?"

"Affirmative on that, too."

"So? I'm waiting."

"Tall, slender, dark hair, clean shaven except for a thin moustache. How's that?"

"That's the same description I got from Mr. Reynolds down at the Bootery. He had sold a pair of Hessian boots to that same Jessie Scout."

"You mean all my efforts, all that tearing around at General McClellan's headquarters to get a pass was all for naught?"

"Bert, don't be so hard on yourself. I appreciate everything you did for me."

"I had hoped to help you or thought I could help you."

"Bert, did Sorenson give you any reason for not coming forward with this information before? He must have read about the murder in the paper."

"I asked him about that. He told me the Jessie Scout asked him to say nothing and to close this gentleman's agreement, the Jessie Scout slipped him $20 to keep his mouth shut."

"I don't understand," Jenny said. "If Sorenson had been bribed to remain silent, why would he suddenly open up to you?"

"I gave him $35."

"Bert, you didn't!"

"Oh yes, I did."

"What were you thinking?"

"I thought that if the sheriff ever captured the Jessie Scout, this guy Sorenson would make a damned good witness and we'd have a good case against the murderer."

"I never thought of it that way."

"Aren't you going to offer me at least a cup of tea or something for all my labors?"

"Of course, I will. Come into the kitchen."

CHAPTER VII

When Michel came to pick Jenny up in the morning, she noticed he wasn't wearing the full Union Army blue. His overcoat was blue, but the jacket underneath was Confederate grey. Her eyes flicked over the jacket searching for a missing button, but every one was in place. Then the trousers were the regulation blue. On his feet were cavalry boots.

"Are you in disguise, Michel?"

"Because of this mismatched jacket and pants? Chérie, we will be passing through Federal lines and I always like to be prepared. Then I need the Confederate jacket to move through rebel lines."

"Where did you get that Confederate jacket?"

"Is that what's bothering you? If I told you I had it, you would think I were a traitor, wouldn't you?"

She was silent but was beginning to wonder if going with him, after all, was a mistake.

"The truth is I own this jacket. It belongs to me. I have a couple more at home, too. Two friends in the Union Army gave them to me."

"Where did they get them?"

"What I have to say is not pleasant, ma chére."

Jenny braced herself for the worst.

"You're sure you want to hear this?"

"Yes. Yes, I do."

"They removed these jackets from the dead bodies of Confederates on the battlefield. Remember when the Union thought it had won the Battle of Manassas? At that interlude, until the South's victory, my two friends - not only them; others did the same, too - stripped the bodies of Confederate dead of their uniforms, watches, and who knows what else."

Jenny shuddered.

"Chérie, the Confederates do the same to the Feds, especially, if the Yankees are wearing some good boots or shoes. Those are prize items.

"The next couple of hours," Michel explained, "we'll be riding on the periphery of a Union encampment."

Michel realized she was upset. "Would you prefer returning home?"

"No."

"No? Nothing else?" Michel asked.

"It's hard for me to speak while riding a horse at the same time."

"I understand. Do you feel all right?"

"Yes."

"Do you feel well enough to continue our journey?"

"Yes."

"I see you're not wearing the bracelet today," Michel said.

"No, not on a day where we go into rebel territory."

"You're right - it would be asking for trouble. I hope you're keeping it in a safe place."

"I think it is. It's in the top drawer of my dresser."

"Do you still like it, chérie?"

"I love it."

He smiled at her.

Jenny thought for a minute, then asked, "Michel, I want to ask you something about the bracelet."

"Is there something wrong? Is a diamond missing? Did one fall out?"

"No, it's intact."

"Eh bien, what?"

"I was just curious where you bought it."

He studied her, his eyes cagey. "Wouldn't I buy you only the best?"

"I know that, Michel, but this is so extraordinarily beautiful that I find it difficult to believe that you bought it around here. Maybe in New York."

"It was in New York. Perhaps you noted the inscription 'To A.T. from R.T.' on it."

"Yes, I did." She felt a warm flush break out over her face and turned away so he wouldn't see her reaction.

"Chérie, stop. You don't have to be embarrassed about a question."

"Michel -"

"Don't say a word, chérie. I'll tell you where I bought it. I should have told you before. Yes, I did buy it in New York - in a pawn shop."

"Oh." She didn't expect that.

"Perhaps you don't know, but pawn shops have some very expensive stuff for sale. Someone, apparently, was desperate for cash and I was fortunate to come along and get a good buy."

"Thank you for telling me, Michel."

"You have tears in your eyes. Did I do that to you? Forgive me, ma chére." He hugged her. "You know, when I bought the bracelet and saw the inscription, I didn't like it because I felt the bracelet would never seem to be yours, truly yours, but it was so beautiful I couldn't resist. Then I thought those initials could be scratched out, but then that would mar the beauty of the bracelet. So now you know. Feel better about that?"

"Yes, thank you, Michel." She wondered if Mrs. Martin would accept the pawn shop story; it sounded plausible. But when did Michel go to New York and why? The real why. She was afraid to ask.

"Should we continue our journey?" he asked.

She nodded.

There was a rustle of something or someone coming through the brush.

"Sh-h, don't move," Michel said. He placed a hand on hers. "Wait." Hoofbeats followed.

Suddenly four Federal soldiers, accompanied by a sergeant, burst on the scene, guns pointed directly at Michel and Jenny.

"Stop or we'll shoot," the sergeant said.

"What is the meaning of this?" demanded Michel.

"Don't you know what a gun means, Mister?" the sergeant asked. The four privates guffawed.

"How dare you capture a U.S. soldier in his own lines?" asked Michel.

"Who says you're a U.S. soldier - you?" the sergeant asked. His men laughed.

"Surely, you must know me, recognize me," Michel said. The men looked at one another, shaking their heads, shrugging their shoulders.

"Don't you men belong to General Grigg's Cavalry?" The ring of command was in Michel's voice.

"Yes, we do," they said in unison.

"Well, don't you remember seeing me at headquarters?"

"I think you're a spy," the sergeant said, "using that young woman as a decoy."

"I could have you hanged for your insubordination, Sergeant. Do you know that?" asked Michel.

"It's easy for you to say who you are so you can get into our lines dressed in our uniform coat," the sergeant said, "but let's see the kind of pants you're wearing."

Jenny noted that, thus far, no uniform had been visible on either side except the blue overcoats and the high cavalry boots.

"How do I know you are who you say you are?" Michel said. "Let's see the pants you're wearing first."

"All right," the sergeant said. "Men, show this impostor the pants you're wearing."

The Union soldiers threw back their coats and showed regulation regimental blue trousers.

"Now," the sergeant said to Michel, "let's see the trousers you're wearing; if you can, that is."

Carefully keeping his grey jacket covered with his blue overcoat, Michel revealed U.S. Army trousers, but with the stripe of a commissioned officer. The Yankees stared at it. Michel's tone quickly became authoritative. "You see, you have insulted an officer."

The four privates turned to go, but the sergeant stopped them. "Wait a minute. There's something fishy about this guy."

Jenny felt her heart throb in her throat. She feared for Michel as well as for herself.

Michel drew himself up to his full height. "Fishy, is there? Sergeant, come right along with me to headquarters and I'll get my satisfaction yet before I'm through with you. I'll teach you a lesson you'll long remember."

The soldiers quickly turned away and left.

Jenny waited till the men were well out of sight and the hoofbeats had receded. "Michel, you were magnificent. What a perfomance! But you spoke like an American, not a Frenchman."

"You forget, chérie, I'm an actor."

"You sure had me fooled," Jenny said, "just like they were."

"If you think that's anything, you should see me do Hamlet with an English accent."

"Have you done *Hamlet* recently?"

"No. The last Shakespearean play I did was *Richard III* where I portrayed the Duke of Clarence. But the character of Hamlet is much more versatile, compelling the actor to span the entire range of human emotions."

As they continued on their way, Jenny found herself chuckling over how Michel had tricked the soldiers.

"Michel, but you are in the Union Army, so even if you had revealed yourself, it wouldn't be so bad, would it?"

"Chérie, I'm wearing a Confederate jacket to get us into rebel lines and how could I explain that to those guys? You could see and feel the sergeant and his men were on a hunting expedition...hunting for rebels, that is."

Is Michel a dangerous man? Is there a darker side to him she knows nothing about? Is her life on the line just being with him? He seems to know the route pretty well; she wondered how often he has traversed it. In whose behalf? The North or the South?

He carries no gun. If they are challenged again, how would he protect her? Maybe next time he wouldn't be able to pull off that clever stunt she had just witnessed.

"Where are we headed now?" she asked, a bit uneasy.

"To General Beauregard's headquarters." He caught her change of mood. "Do you think I'd lead you astray?"

"The journey seems long."

"Are you tiring? We can stop and rest awhile, if you wish."

"No. I'm just kind of on edge about moving around these encampments, whether Union or Confederate."

They followed a well-beaten path that pitched them into a forest. The trees were so dense they blocked out all light. Was it only minutes ago that the sun blazed overhead? Now it was like an eclipse had occurred and night had descended.

She was apprehensive, not knowing who might pop out at them. She had placed implicit faith in Michel and hoped that wasn't a misplaced trust.

"How much further did you say it was?" Jenny asked.

"A little more ways yet."

Her mind was doing all kinds of flipflops: is Michel really taking her to see Beauregard? Is he a bona fide intelligence agent or a renegade?

Why was she suddenly thinking of things like this? With no one around to come to her aid, how would she, could she manage against a possibly dangerous man? He's on familiar ground and in control of the situation. She knew that and already had seen him perform before those Federals. Very clever the way he had done that, but there might not be a next time.

Her eyes darted from left to right, searching, combing, and scrutinizing the underbrush. "Would a sniper lurk here?" she asked fearfully.

"If there is one," said Michel, "he'd more likely be in a tree, higher up, so he'd get a better vantage point and also could conceal his own presence." Michel watched her. "Chérie, don't look so alarmed. You're safe with me. I'm here to protect you and I won't let anything happen to you, so relax."

"You don't have a gun."

"See what happened when we were challenged by that Federal sergeant? Relax. You have nothing to worry about."

"Was I talking too loud before those men came upon us?"

"No."

Ahead of them was a clearing, out of the forest and the darkness into the light of bright sunshine.

"Let's speak low," Michel said.

She nodded, too frightened to reply.

Then a voice rang out, "Halt. Who goes there?"

She trembled.

Michel placed a finger over his lips.

Out loud, he shouted, "A friend."

"Advance, friend, and give the countersign."

"Stay here, Jenny. I'll be right back." She watched him as he moved forward to speak to the guard. Whatever Michel said to let them pass through, Jenny couldn't hear because his voice was inaudible.

He motioned to her to come forward. Before entering General Beauregard's headquarters, Michel removed the Federal overcoat.

The General chuckled when he observed the gray jacket over the blue pants. "We're going to have to get you grey pants to go with that jacket, mon ami."

"Mon Général, I'd like to introduce you to Mademoiselle Jennifer Edwards."

"Enchanté, mademoiselle," General Beauregard said, kissing her hand. "What would you like to ask me?"

"General, can you tell me how you so easily defeated the Feds at Bull Run?"

"You mean Manassas?"

"Yes."

"Of course, I can't be too specific because I might use this plan again in the future."

"You were called the hero of Fort Sumter. Is it true that you were told to act on the defensive at Manassas?"

"Yes. I was the commander of the Alexandrian Line. The Union Army had crossed the Potomac and occupied Alexandria, Virginia."

"How many men did you command then?"

"About 6,000. I had the troops stretched all the way from Manassas to the fords of the Bull Run stream. Another group controlled a position at Centreville. I felt my force was too thinly distributed and that it would be difficult to hold that line so I asked President Davis for 10,000 more men. I knew if I didn't get them, I would have to retreat towards Richmond. But I did, in the end, obtain the number of men I requested."

"Wasn't there also a problem as to how Confederates could be distinguished from Federals," asked Jenny, "since many of them were wearing Federal jackets or pants at the time?"

"Yes, that's correct. I thought a better idea would be for my men to wear colored scarves, red on one side, yellow on the other, which would extend from shoulder to waist."

"Not white?" asked Jenny.

"White is for the Jessie Scouts, isn't it, Michel?"
He looked in Michel's direction and Michel nodded.

"We wouldn't want to be associated with that bunch, since they're Feds spying on us. Besides, I don't think your General Fremont would appreciate that, if we confused the issue by wearing a white scarf. He was the one who named these scouts in the first place, in honor of his wife, Jessie. Crazy idea.

"Back to my scarves. President Davis thought my idea wouldn't work. He'd have to have a lot of Confederate women make the scarves, he said, and that presented complications. Also, President Davis thought my identity symbols were much too large and he suggested and ordered that rosettes were a better choice."

"Facing the Feds then," said Jenny, "what were the first things you did?"

"We began to build fortifications around Manassas. It was imperative for us to hold the town and all of its railroad connections. If it hadn't been for the courier service of Rose O'Neal Greenhow, we wouldn't have known when McDowell and his men were going to begin their march on Manassas. You've heard of Mrs. Greenhow, haven't you, mademoiselle?"

"Oh yes, she's in jail now."

"Pity. Well, she had a very fine courier." He turned his head and winked at Michel. "And if it hadn't been for him with that message, we might not have had the victory."

"I heard that a lot of Southern girls from Virginia kept the Confederate command posted as to the movements of the Federals."

"Yes, they did, but it was the Northern newspapers that were especially helpful with details about troops, their strength, deployment, and command. Michel kept me supplied with a number of Northern newspapers."

Jenny frowned.

General Beauregard said, "No, no, mademoiselle, don't worry about Michel. He's a good soldier. Michel and I go way back and our friendship goes beyond man-made boundaries or politics, n'est-ce pas, mon ami?" He slapped Michel on the back.

"There was a time at Bull Run," Jenny said, "I mean Manassas, when war correspondents returned from the battlefield and bragged that you, General, had been pushed to the wall."

"That was laughable, especially when Northern papers came out with their extras that the war was already over and the North had won. One of your ministers in Washington said the reason the North lost was because they fought the battle on a Sunday, the Lord's Day. But does that mean that we in the South are heathens because we won?" The General winked at Michel and both of them threw their heads back and laughed heartily.

"Can you give me your battle strategy, General?" Jenny asked again.

"I can't tell you too much as I stated before, but I can tell you what didn't work. My strategy was strictly Napoleonic. My original plan called for an attack on Centreville to be delivered by four brigades: two brigades moving from the center, and two brigades from the left. Six brigades were to cross the fords of the Bull Run stream on the right and support the attack on Centreville."

"But you said this didn't work in the end?" Jenny asked.

"That's right. This great military plan could not be executed."

"Why was that?"

"At about 5:00 o'clock in the morning, we heard gunfire break out on our left. Then we learned that reenforcements from General Johnston hadn't arrived yet. But when they did eventually, we launched an all out offensive."

"One of the Northern correspondents said you were riding a headless horse in the midst of battle."

Beauregard laughed. "I don't know how I could do that. When you figure out how that feat could be accomplished, let me know. I did have a horse killed under me, but I substituted another and wound up riding a captured Federal horse."

"Finally, General: can you sum up what you feel is your principle of waging war?"

"In a word, one of mass of concentration of force. The whole science of war may be briefly defined as the art of placing in the right position at the right time, a mass of troops greater than that of your enemy."

"Thank you, General, for your time."

"My pleasure, mademoiselle. Michel, can I see you some time in the next day or so?"

"Bien. Of course, you'll be here?"

The General nodded. Then, "Au revoir, mademoiselle."

"That was wonderful, Michel! I can hardly wait to get back to Washington to write this up."

"Did you get enough material?"

"Plenty. Thanks so much for a chance of a lifetime of a great story with a very dynamic man. Sounds like you and the General share a few secrets," said Jenny.

"That's what makes life interesting, chérie. I'm sure you have a few secrets of your own, n'est-ce pas?" He held up his hand. "No, no don't tell me. Keep your secrets, ma chére. That's what makes you so exciting to a man like me."

With that, he turned his attention to the route that led them back to Washington.

As they approached Jenny's home, she was surprised to see Sheriff

MacKenzie standing at her door.

"What does he want?" Michel asked.

"I don't know."

"Jenny, don't tell him where you were today. Understand?"

"Sure, but why?"

"I'll tell you later."

"So what should I say where I've been?"

"Tell him we went out for a ride, had a picnic. Mon Dieu! Look - you're a writer. You can make up something, can't you?"

She was puzzled by the sudden testiness. "Michel, are you angry with me?"

"No, not with you."

"What then?"

"Every time you and I turn around, the sheriff is always there, like an uninvited guest at a wedding."

"I told you he's a friend and is as interested in my welfare as you are."

"You know, Jenny, if Sheriff MacKenzie would spend more time in the office instead of chasing after you, he might solve the murder case."

"Why, Michel - you're jealous!"

"I'm not jealous. You said yourself he's old enough to be your father."

He leaned forward and mumbled. "I'm going to my home now. Don't forget what I told you. Au revoir."

Jenny watched him ride away and even wave to the sheriff as he passed by the house.

"Sheriff, have you been waiting long?"

"I got here five minutes ago. Where have you been? I had stopped at Laura's and she didn't know where you were, either."

"We had a picnic and went out for a ride."

"Really? Where's your picnic basket?"

Jenny blushed. "I thought Michel had taken it. Come on into the house, Sheriff. Can I offer you a cup of tea?"

"That would be fine."

"Make yourself comfortable. What's new with the case?"

"That's what I came over to tell you."

"Good news?"

"I thought you'd like to know I had written to Edwin Booth in

New York to verify Michel's alibi. He answered very promptly."

"What did he say?"

"He confirmed everything, including Michel's times for curtain calls and attendance at the cast party. Also, the approximate times that Michel gave for leaving the theater were more accurate than even I would have imagined. Booth corroborated all the times, most of them being no more than 15 or 20 minutes off from what Michel gave me.

"That time that Michel gave for the curtain calls, for instance, is locked up so tightly there just doesn't seem to be any way he could have been at the murder scene September 24."

"So then you're satisfied with Michel's alibi?"

"I see no other way. There's no proof, not even an inkling that Michel was involved in anything that might affect the murder."

"Why were you so determined to hang a guilty plea on Michel?"

"Jennifer, don't be so sensitive. I did that with everyone. Bert Wells, for example. I asked would it be possible for him to have been at the murder scene? The answer was negative because he was in Harrisburg, Pennsylvania."

"I see. What surprises me, Sheriff, is that you didn't work out who had the motive first."

"Frankly, I never seemed to be able to."

"Sheriff, have you now arrived at the motive of the Jessie Scout who had killed Todd and struck me?"

"No, I still haven't. I can't make a definitive statement about that."

"Well, perhaps I can help you: Bert Wells dropped in the other day to tell me he had tracked down the company in which Todd had served."

"What was the point of that?"

"Martha had mentioned that Todd had seen a Jessie Scout eavesdropping near an officer's tent. When the officer left, the Jessie Scout barged into the tent, grabbed some papers from the officer's desk and dashed out. But he encountered Todd and when Todd had challenged him, he socked him and Todd fell to the ground."

"Why didn't Martha give me these details?"

"Sheriff, you never asked her what she thought was the motive."

"O.K., go ahead."

"Bert was sure that someone had witnessed this and he found a private by the name of Phillip Sorenson."

"And had he seen the attack on Todd?"

"Oh yes, and he told Bert that the Jessie Scout asked him to help move Todd's body away from the officer's tent, which he did."

"Did this Phillip Sorenson get a look at the Jessie Scout?"

"He did. Todd also got a good look at the Jessie Scout, too, and that's why Martha thinks Todd was killed."

"What kind of a description do you have?"

"Unfortunately, the description of the Jessie Scout Bert gave me that Sorenson gave him is the same as that given by Mr. Reynolds of the Bootery."

"Which is?"

"Tall, dark hair, pencil thin moustache, otherwise clean-shaven. You had considered that before as incomplete, remember, Sheriff?"

"I still do. Jennifer, tell me why this guy didn't come forward with this item?"

"Because the Jessie Scout paid him off to keep his mouth shut."

"But he talked to Bert finally," said the sheriff.

"Bert gave him $35 to open up and he did."

"Well, now after listening to your story, I can see why the Jessie Scout killed Todd because he didn't want to be identified as a spy. He wears the Jessie Scout uniform to pretend he's spying on the Confederates for the Union. In reality, he's really spying on the Feds for the rebels. He's got a nice little racket going. - I wonder how much they're paying him?"

"Sheriff, wouldn't it be possible that he might be a double spy; that is, working for both Union and Confederacy?"

"Maybe. For the present, that might be difficult to prove."

"If he's only spying on the Feds for the rebels, that's very frightening," said Jenny. "Based on that theory and his motive for killing Todd, then what would be the motive for striking at me?"

"I don't know because if we use the same reasoning, namely so that you wouldn't be able to identify your assailant, that doesn't make much sense."

"Why not?"

"The most important reason is he was wearing a bandanna to conceal his face, so how could you identify him, if in some twisted, convoluted way you even knew him?"

"Then the no-motive was merely the fact I was there and in the way."

"At the moment, that's all I can assume.
Jennifer, I wish you and Bert would stop playing amateur detective.
Bert should have come directly to me with all this information. There's no reason why I have to get these details secondhand."

"Are you angry, Sheriff?"

"I'm not angry but annoyed. I've warned you not to do any investigative work on your own because you're not equipped to do so and the end result will be you're going to get hurt. You might pass this message on to Bert, while you're at it."

"And if we latch on to a clue, then what?"

"Tell me and I'll take over. Besides, don't you think we should share any information because we're both interested in solving this crime. What can you say for yourself now, Jennifer?"

"Would you like another cup of tea?"

"No thanks. I'll head back to the office."

After the sheriff left, Jenny sat down to write her interview with General Beauregard. Some of the observations she made she wouldn't be able to include in her story.

When Michel first told her about going, he referred to Bull Run as Manassas. She knew that only a dyed-in-the-wool Southerner would call the Battle of Bull Run Manassas.

Then Michel addressed Beauregard as, "Mon Général".
Was that merely a sign of respect, or is he really serving under the General? Those secret missions he keeps referring to all the time: is that for our side or the other side?

Least of all, was that wink that Beauregard gave Michel significant when he spoke about the courier that saved the day and gave him the victory he wanted at Bull Run?

As for bringing Northern newspapers to Beauregard to read - well, that isn't exactly a crime. Freedom of the press is still alive and well and that goes for the distribution of the papers.

Finally, how come Michel knew the password when the Confederate sentry challenged him?

Just a couple of niggling things that troubled her, although she was sure that there was a reasonable explanation for all of them, she hoped, just like the reasonable explanation for the inscription of the bracelet and how it came in his possession.

Three sharp raps on the door broke into her reverie.

"Chérie, am I still welcome here?"

"Of course, you are. Come in."

"Are you all right, chérie?"

"Yes, I'm fine."

"What did the sheriff say?"

"He wanted to know where the picnic hamper was, if we went on a picnic as I claimed."

"How did you answer that?"

"I told him you had probably taken it."

"Is that all?"

"Just about. Michel, why didn't you want me to tell the truth where we were?"

"Because we'd get into trouble crossing into rebel lines. We could be arrested for being Confederate sympathizers."

"The sheriff will eventually know when I write up my interview."

"Do as I say, without question," he ordered.

For a moment, she caught a glimpse of another Michel - demanding, ruthless, volatile.

"Besides, you're on the Union side," she said finally.

"That's true, but still, I'm wearing a Confederate jacket. It would open us up to too many questions."

"You can prove who you are without any repercussions, can't you?"

"I can, but I don't like to."

"Because you're doing undercover work?"

"Exactly. I'm disappointed the sheriff didn't throw any more light on the case."

"Oh, he did. He told me he had written Edwin Booth to substantiate your alibi."

"And what did my friend Eddie have to say?"

"He concurred with everything you stated."

"Glad to hear that. I hope that keeps the sheriff satisfied and away for awhile, a long while."

CHAPTER VIII

"Jenny, how would you like to do a story from the inside of a balloon gondola?" asked Bert.

"I don't know. I've never been in a balloon before." He's probably trying to make amends for the time lost at General Sherman's, she thought. "Wait a minute -what do you know about ballooning, Bert?"

"I was trained as an aeronaut by Thaddeus Lowe. There were others, too, along with me. We were to remain civilians, but paid by the government. That was the way it was supposed to be."

"What would an aeronaut do?"

"We'd watch the enemy from the balloon and then make maps of what we saw."

"How would you communicate with the officer in charge if you saw something suspicious?"

"Professor Lowe wanted a telegraph on board every balloon."

"So what happened to your great high-flying career?"

"It just didn't catch on. Secretary Cameron and President Lincoln were very impressed and thought the idea of a Balloon Corps to use in the war against the South had great possibilities, but General Scott couldn't have cared less. A lot of other people thought the balloon concept was worthless. I didn't think there was much of a future for me in this; besides, I wanted to continue to be a reporter and war correspondent."

"But where will you get a balloon for joy riding?"

"Professor Lowe and I became great friends and he told me that if I ever wanted to take a balloon up to show someone what I could do, he'd let me use one of his.

"I told him you were going to do a feature on it and he approved - the more publicity the better. He felt that the more people we could get to ride in the balloon, the faster we could spread the word how the balloon could be used in war as well as in peace. He seems to think that next year Lincoln will use his influence to put the balloon in the war. Are you interested or not?"

"Interested, yes, but kind of scared, too."

"You don't have to be afraid if you're with someone like me who knows all the ins and outs of navigating. I got a great idea: why don't you invite Laura to come with us, too?"

"Is there enough room in that gondola?"

"Three people are the limit. When you speak to Laura, remind her that you both will have to get up early in the morning, unless that bothers you."

"No, for a good story I'll do anything - well, within reason."

"I've got some guys who will pump the balloon full of gas at our take-off point."

"How will the balloon get there?"

"You'll see. These guys come in a buckboard. The balloon is tied to the back of it and then the wagon itself has all the equipment we need to take with us."

At 5:00 A.M. the next morning Laura and Jenny shivered in the pre-dawn air outside Washington, as they watched the men fill the balloon with hydrogen.

"Come on, girls," Bert called. "Climb aboard. Glad to see you're wearing sweaters. You'll need them when we go aloft."

Then it was time for lift-off. As the balloon floated slowly heavenward, a gentle wind nudged it to the west.

"It's chilly up here," Jenny said.

"There's the White House, Jenny, over there, look," Laura said. "Isn't that Michel running towards us?" She pointed to the ground below.

"I wonder what he's up to," Jenny said.

"No good, probably," said Bert.

"Bert, look he's signalling to us. He wants us to come back."

"Nothing doing. That's just a pretext to get you down. Is that guy going to follow you from now till Kingdom Come?"

"Maybe he's got an urgent message," Jenny said.

"Sure. He wants a ride. I'm not turning back - take it or leave it."

"Bert, he would never have come here if he didn't have something important to say," said Jenny.

"Sorry, I'm not biting."

"You won't go back?" Jenny asked. "We're so close to our starting point, why couldn't we just drop in quickly and then fly off again?"

"Oh, just like that, huh?" Bert snapped his fingers.

"Why not? It seems so simple," said Jenny.

"Let me get this straight: you want me to turn around, pull the rope that lets the gas out -"

"Why would you want to do that?" interrupted Jenny.

"Do you have a better way to land? As I was saying - pull the rope that lets the gas out, land, so your darling can speak to you."

"Bert, Michel wouldn't come here to ask us to turn around on a mere whim."

"Want to bet? It took two hours just to inflate this balloon and now you want me to land, find out what Michel wants - which is nothing - and then what? Spend another two hours reinflating the balloon?"

"Don't give me that baloney about two hours,"
said Jenny. "I saw your helpers using a machine to inflate. You're not exactly blowing the balloon up by yourself."

"Shows you how much you know about this procedure. The men were using a field generator, an invention of Professor Lowe's. But even using that doesn't speed up the process. It still takes two hours to inflate. If we stop now to deflate in order to land, you can count on two hours lost to reinflate to get back up in the air, and then you might as well forget about going for the ride."

"Why are you such a crab?" asked Jenny.

"You'd be a crab, too, if you knew what was at stake."

"Like what?"

"The wind, for one thing. We had just the right amount when we got started this morning. Besides, the guys that helped us launch are no longer around. I can't get this off the ground and back up in the air without assistance."

"I didn't know that," she said.

He looked at her.

"Conditions for the flight can and do change. That's why we leave early in the morning because usually weather and wind velocity are perfect for take-off. I can't imagine what's so earthshaking for Michel to interrupt our schedule. All I know is there weren't any newsboys hawking extras before we left. Whatever Michel has to say won't affect our country and can wait till we return."

"Will you two stop arguing and look at the view. You're missing everything," said Laura.

"What a view is right!" Jenny said. "Look down over there to the right, Laura. See him? Where's that guy going? What's he doing?"

"He's holding up that wagon train," Bert said. "He's wearing a Confederate uniform. I didn't think we had drifted that fast into enemy territory."

Jenny stared at the Jessie Scout below. His face was concealed with a bandanna, like that other Jessie Scout in her memory. First came a chill, then numbness as fear set in, the fear of an impending attack that continued to control her, distort and twist her judgment.

It was there down below with its terror spelled out in the white kerchief hanging down over the shoulder of the Jessie Scout. The nightmare began to replay from deep within the recesses of her lost memory. But try as she might, she couldn't rid herself of the emotions that overwhelmed her, pushing her into a panic.

When will the anguish stop? Will she ever purge herself of this misery? She saw him stalk her all over again. Bert stared at her, not quite understanding what he saw.

"Every time Jenny sees a Jessie Scout," explained Laura, "it brings back memories of her attack."

"I see. Because her assailant was a Jessie Scout?"

"Yes."

"How will she ever get control of these emotions?"

"Hopefully, in time."

"What can we do to bring her around?"

"Nothing. She has to play the whole thing through and then recover from the trauma on her own."

"It's like she's in a trance," Bert said. He raised his hand to slap her. Laura couldn't stop him in time.

Jenny slid to the floor of the gondola, trying to evade another attack on her person, covering her head with her hands, her whole body leaning forward in anticipation of the oncoming attack.

"No," she screeched. "Stop it."

"You shouldn't have done that," Laura said. "That doesn't help the situation."

"I thought it would. I can't stand around here, so utterly helpless, unable to do anything for Jenny."

"Well, can you see what happened? She's still back there at the attack scene. Now she's trying to protect herself from another blow."

"I didn't know," said Bert.

He was on his knees, looking into her face. He pulled her gently to her feet. "Are you all right, Jenny?"

She opened her eyes, dazed. For a minute she was disoriented and began to sway. Two strong arms steadied her.

As if brought back from another world, she looked dumbly at Bert, then at Laura.

"What's the matter, Jenny?" Laura asked.

"Just those demons haunting me again."

"Feel better now?" Bert asked.

"Yes, much. Are we still on the Union side?"

"Yes," Laura said. "There's a United States flag on the wagon. Do you see it?"

"I see it now. Bert, look, the Jessie Scout is pointing a gun at the driver. Here comes another Jessie Scout, too. The driver won't leave his perch. Oh no, that first Jessie Scout pushed the driver to the ground and struck him with the butt of his gun. You see that? Bert, do something! Can't we yell?"

"Great idea - what will that accomplish? Then they'll start shooting at us. That's all we need."

"How can they shoot this far up?"

"Jenny," Bert reminded her, "and what could you do even if you were down there below with those bandits?"

"That poor driver. No one is coming to help him. They're taking over the wagon train. I wonder what the cargo is," Laura said.

"Jenny, look! Those two Jessie Scouts have removed the white kerchiefs and are tying them around their necks."

"Bert, can we follow those guys and find out where they're going?" asked Jenny.

"I don't want to get caught in enemy territory. But only for a little ways. Let's see what will happen."

"Bert, how high up are we, do you know?"

"About 300 feet."

"But we can't do anything to stop those robbers, can we?"

"Too dangerous. Even if we were to drop in on them, they have guns and could start shooting at us."

"Let's follow them anyway. I wonder where they're going."

"Looks to me like they're headed for Virginia," Bert said.

"It's so quiet and peaceful up here and so easy to forget about the war," Laura said.

The wagon train below had stopped and then as if on signal, hundreds of Confederate soldiers poured out of a stand of trees and ran towards it. Some of the men were shaking hands with the Jessie Scouts; others were digging into the cargo of the wagon train.

"Laura, look there were shoes on that wagon train. The way those guys are grabbing the shoes, you'd think they had never seen shoes before."

"Yeah," Bert said, "I've heard from an anonyomous source that the rebels have a shortage of shoes and some of the soldiers go barefoot."

"Even in battle?" asked Jenny.

"That's what I was told. I bet this wagon train originated in Lynn, Massachusetts. That's where the shoes for the Union Army are being manufactured."

"Jenny", Laura said, tapping her on her hand, "look what's going on down there."

Then they heard a noise like thunder.

"Is that a storm coming?" asked Jenny, her eyes sweeping the sky.

"If you two would stop gabbing," Bert said, "and look below, you'd see those guys are getting ready to shoot their cannon at us. You're looking in the wrong direction, it's to the right."

"They'll blow us away," said Jenny.

"What happens if they hit the gondola?" asked Laura.

"We'll be O.K. on that," said Bert, "because the floor has been fitted with heavy armorplate and that should protect us from bullets fired from the ground. Let's stop talking and get out of here."

"But how?" Laura asked.

"By doing this," Bert said, as he threw out some stuff from the gondola.

"What are you doing?" asked Jenny.

"We have to go higher and so we have to lighten our load." He was interrupted by a boom from the cannon. By that time they were beginning to ascend and the salvo missed them.

Bert yelled at Jenny. "We're not moving fast enough. Cut loose one of those 100 lb. bags of sand tied to the side of the gondola."

"Where? How? I can't. What are you talking about? They're still shooting at us."

"Stop asking questions and do as you're told," Bert shouted.

"I can't," Jenny said.

"What do you mean you can't? Can't you see I'm busy now trying to get away? We've got to get higher to elude them or they will continue to use us for target practice."

"Stop yelling at me!"

"For heavens' sakes, Jenny, this is no time for ceremony, it's time for action! Cut the bag!"

"I don't have a knife," Jenny said. "Do you?"

"I thought I did," Bert said, checking his pants pockets. "You'll have to do the best you can, but hurry up, will you?"

"Jenny, I've got a small nail scissors in my purse. Will that help? It will be a slow process."

"I can't figure out where I put that knife," Bert said. "Well, do the best you can."

"Laura, duck."

"I'm cutting one of those bags."

"Hurry. They're starting to fire the cannon again."

"I found it," Bert yelled. "Must have fallen out of my pocket. Hang on, ladies!" He quickly cut loose two 100 lb. sand bags and as if by magic, the balloon sailed up and away from the shooting below.

"See how simple it is?" said Bert.

"It's simple, all right," said Jenny. "We almost got killed."

"When you want to climb further, just get rid of the weights," Bert said.

"Scared us half to death on the way," said Jenny.

"Maybe we can relax now," said Laura, "and enjoy the ride and scenery."

"I'm beginning to like this," said Jenny.

"Jenny," Laura said, "I can't forget those two Jessie Scouts that held up the wagon train. But why did they have to bludgeon the driver?"

"I see how those Jessie Scouts can fool a lot of people," Jenny said. "Dressed in Confederate uniforms, they can pass for rebels, but when in Federal land, they know that white kerchief spread on their shoulder labels them as spies for the Union and no one will bother them. That is what they want people to think."

"These men couldn't be real Jessie Scouts, unless they're renegades, because the real Jessie Scouts are valuable to our side and they certainly wouldn't commit any crime." Laura said.

"They must have been renegades," Jenny said. "It doesn't make any sense for Jessie Scouts to hold up a wagon train headed for Federal Headquarters with a load of shoes for the Union Army then change direction and give the shoes to the South."

"Then I wonder," Laura said, "if that Jessie Scout who attacked you was a renegade."

"He had a score to settle," Jenny replied, "and I don't think that had anything to do with the uniform he was wearing."

"It could be that one of those scouts down there was your Jessie Scout, Jenny," Laura said.

"Who's her Jessie Scout?" Bert asked.

"The guy who attacked her," Laura said.

"I don't know," said Jenny. "I think I'm ready to go home. I've had enough ballooning to last me for a lifetime."

"Looks like we're over Union territory," Bert announced. "See the soldiers down there all dressed in blue?"

"A sight for sore eyes. I can hardly wait to get down," Jenny said.

Bert pulled on a rope. "Now we're letting out some of the gas from the balloon. Get ready to land, girls. Hang on."

"The soldiers see us," said Jenny. "Laura, wave to them."

"Hey, they're shooting at us! Real friendly types, aren't they?"

"They think we're the enemy," said Jenny. "Bert, do something! Can we get higher and away from them? We're sinking awfully fast!"

"I'll see what I can do," said Bert.

"Don't just see, Bert, do something! Laura, duck! Laura, whatever are you doing?" asked Jenny.

"I have a white handkerchief," Laura said, fraantically waving.

"We're going to be killed," said Jenny. "Let's get out of here."

"That's what I'm trying to do," Bert said. "Be patient. Laura, for heavens' sakes, what are you doing?"

"I'm going to surrender so that they'll stop shooting at us."

"Laura," said Jenny, "you're going to fall out of the gondola. You're leaning out too far. Bert, why are we falling?"

"We're going to land."

"No," Jenny said. "Not here. The soldiers will start shooting."

"They didn't pay any attention to my white flag of surrender," Laura said.

"Hold on," Bert said, "this landing could be kind of bumpy."

"Bert, watch out. Ouch. You just hit that tree."

"That was only the top and that's a sign of a good landing."

"Who said that?" asked Jenny. "I don't believe you. Do you know what you're doing?"

Jenny and Laura grabbed the sides of the gondola and watched as the ground raced to meet them. Both girls closed their eyes, expecting the worst.

As soon as they landed, the Union soldiers surrounded them, their rifles pointed at them.

"Now don't get hasty, gentlemen," Bert said. "Don't do something you'll be sorry for. I can explain everything."

"I hope you can," said Jenny.

The buckboard with the crew had already arrived, waiting to dismantle the balloon and load it back on the wagon.

"Did you get enough material for a feature, Jenny?" Bert asked.

"Oh yes."

"What will you use as the focus of your article?"

"I'm torn between two leads: from being blown out of the sky by a cannon or trying to land with my life threatened by soldiers with rifles at the ready. A difficult choice."

"If the Union Generals had only believed in the balloon," Bert said, "General McDowell would have won the Battle of Bull Run because the balloon could have enabled him to see the strength of Beauregard's forces and their deployment."

"Bertram1" An older man pushed his way through the soldiers who had surrounded Bert and Jenny and Laura.

"Professor, what a surprise to see you here! Jenny and Laura, I'd like you to meet Professor Thaddeus Lowe, the man responsible for the wonderful ride we just had. This is Jennifer Edwards and Laura Martin, Professor Lowe."

"Nice to meet you, ladies." The professor doffed his hat after the introduction.

"Professor, we had such an exciting ride. Thank you again," Laura said.

"So - you had an exciting joy ride, did you? Bertram, I want to speak to you."

After the soldiers had been dismissed, Bert walked over to Thaddeus Lowe.

"Professor, what's the problem?"

"My boy, you're the problem. Didn't I make it clear to you I forbade any joy riding in the balloon?"

"You did, but, sir, this wasn't a joy ride."

"With two beautiful women as passengers, what would you call it?"

Bert started to stammer. "I-I thought you told me I could take the balloon up. You gave me permission."

"Now, just wait a minute, young man."

"With any passenger..."

"But not for joy riding."

"That you stated anyone who might disseminate information about the balloon to the public or government."

"That's right. That's what I said."

"Well, Jenny here, is a journalist and planned to do a feature for the STAR....."

"The *Washington Evening Star*?"

"Yes, sir, and I thought that was a pretty good reason to take her up."

"But let me remind you, Bertram, you're also a journalist and you've done next to nothing about writing about the balloon. Talking about it - oh, you're good at that."

"Professor, as you know, my editor has given me an assignment. I'm a war correspondent. But I've been planning to do a balloon story and even interviewing you."

"When I see it, I'll believe it. Where is that young lady? I want to speak to her."

"Jenny, Professor Lowe wants to talk to you."

Jenny and Laura had begun to walk away from the area, but turned back at Bert's call.

"Miss Edwards, in your article, I want you to emphasize the advantages of the balloon in war as well as in peace."

"I've been planning to do that along with some of my own personal impressions today."

"That's fine. Anything else?"

"I'd like to interview you, too. Do you think I can get an appointment at your convenience?"

"Of course, I'll talk to you about that later."

"Bertram, what would you have done if something had happened to the balloon on your flight?" Professor Lowe asked.

"Well, nothing had. I brought it back safe and sound and in one piece."

"Let's suppose you're flying over enemy territory and the Confederates have identified you as an enemy and they wheel out their cannon and start firing. The balloon could easily be destroyed. As an expenenced aeronaut, what could you do?"

"The only thing you can do is cut loose a couple of 100 lb. sand-bags and start an ascent as quickly as possible that will remove you from the site."

"That's right, but in the meantime the enemy has shot holes in the balloon, and Bertram, we don't have enough balloons around to replace those lost in battle yet."

"I understand."

"Furthermore, I have no plans to manufacture any more until I get a definitive answer from Washington that the balloons will be used to their maximum advantage. Maybe when General Scott retires, I hope, at the end of the year, I'll be in a better position to pitch the concept of a balloon corps to the President."

"Yes, sir."

"If we had been able to launch a balloon during the Battle of Bull Run, we would have defeated the South, I'm convinced of that. Unfortunately, no one in the government had the foresight to see it."

"Laura," Jenny said, "look at Bert. He looks like the little boy who got his hand caught in the cookie jar."

"I feel sorry for him that Professor Lowe is bawling him out," said Laura.

"He'll recover," Jenny laughed.

"But, Jenny, he tries so hard to impress you."

"I know that."

CHAPTER IX

"Jenny, what a surprise," said Laura. "How are you doing?"

"Fine."

"And how are you feeling?"

"Pretty good, even though my memory is still fuzzy, which can be aggravating. I came over to share some exciting news with you."

"You're going to marry Michel?"

"No, no. Nothing like that."

"What then?"

"My editor talked to me today. Wants me to do a column."

"But you're already doing a column."

"This will be in addition to that feature. This column will be written under a pseudonym and will deal with exposé."

"Like what?"

"Scandals and items that ordinarily don't make the regular news. Kind of behind-the-scenes stuff."

"How will you get these scoops?"

"At the moment, I don't know, but with a pseudonym, I might have greater access to more sources that could lead me to Todd's murderer and my attacker."

"Be careful, Jenny - you're dealing with a killer."

"Remember when I was brought into the hospital after my attack, you said that my hand was curled around a button from the uniform of my assailant. The sheriff wanted to keep the button for evidence. But, Laura, some Jessie Scout out there is missing a button from his jacket."

"I don't think that evidence will ever be useful," Laura said. "You'd have to search a lot of Confederate jackets to find the one with the missing button. How would you even go about that? Where would you begin? That is, if the murderer is really a Jessie Scout and not a pretender."

"You're right. I recall the sheriff told me that the murderer might have deliberately disguised himself as a Jessie Scout to move about more easily. Who knows?"

"Well, if he's not a genuine Jessie Scout and even if he's a Confederate, how would the sheriff locate the jacket with its missing button?"

"That's the point, Laura; there might be somebody out there who knows about such a jacket and the person who wears it, then decides to come forward and tell it all."

"Jenny, if you start writing articles about this guy," Laura said, "the right people might not even be in town to read them."

"Maybe. It's a chance I have to take."

"But, Jenny, this strategy could put you in danger."

"How? No one knows I'm behind the name and only you and the editor know the true identity. I don't believe I have anything to worry about."

"Almost forgot to tell you the name I'll be using: Personne."

"That's French, isn't it?" asked Laura. "But what does it mean?"

"Nobody."

"Which reminds me, Jenny: if someone has information that can be used in the Personne column, how does he get it to you without your revealing yourself?"

"Easy. The editor has a big sign in front of the newsroom stating that anyone who has some story they think Personne can use, give it to the editor and he will pass it on to the columnist.

* * * *

"   Jenny was in the kitchen when she heard Mon Vieux bark, followed by Bert's yelling, "Shut up, dammit!"

She opened the door. "What's all that racket about?" asked Jenny.

"You still got that dog, I see."

"What's it to you? You don't have to take care of it."

"When are you going to return it to Michel?"

"When I get good and ready."

"Are you going to keep me on your doorstep till the end of the war?"

"Don't tempt me! Come in, come in."

"That's more like it. Hmm. Something smells good."

"Roast chicken. Want to stay for dinner?"

"Yes, thank you."

"Dinner is almost ready - you came just in time."

"I didn't come here with any ulterior motive and I certainly didn't come over for a free meal. I came to see how you are."

"Uh huh."

"Do you want me to leave?"

"No. Come into the dining room and I'll give you a glass of sherry."

"You've got two places set," Bert observed. "Were you expecting someone?"

"You came in, didn't you?"

"How did you know I would even come to the door? Is Michel coming to dinner?"

"No. Michel is out on some kind of intelligence mission for the Feds."

"Well, then, I think I'll take advantage of the situation."

"Where have you been the past few days, Bert?"

"On a train out West. Why? Did you miss me?"

"The sheriff has been looking for you."

"Wonder what he wants."

"I don't know," Jenny said.

"Did you miss me?"

"Yeah, I missed your carping."

"At least we're getting somewhere."

"You should have told the sheriff where you were going and that you had to leave town."

"Why? Has he solved the case?"

"Not that I know," Jenny said. "As the sheriff said, 'Everyone is a suspect,' and he has to keep tabs on those involved."

"That's a standard paragraph most sheriffs make when they don't have anything concrete to offer."

"How do you know? Maybe he has discovered something. Every time he digs up a piece of evidence, he's not going to run over to us and tell us about it."

"I suppose."

"What were you doing out West?"

"Secretary Cameron invited me and representatives of the *Baltimore American*, *Boston Journal*, *Philadelphia Enquirer*, and a couple of other newspapers, like the *Cincinnati Gazette*, to ride with him to the western departments."

"It's about General Fremont, isn't it?" asked Jenny.

"How did you know?"

"Washington is full of rumors."

"But that's not the whole story," Bert said. "Secretary Cameron carried in his pocket an order for Fremont's immediate surrender of his post of command. We were going directly to Fremont."

"What happened when you got there? Would you like more chicken, another roll, potato salad. Here help yourself," Jenny said as she passed the platter to him.

"To get back to your question," Bert explained, "Fremont was less than enthusiastic when he saw all of us. I'm sure he sensed what was going to happen. He and Cameron then rode off by themselves to talk."

"Did Secretary Cameron serve him with notice then?"

"Not exactly. When they came back, Cameron's order was mysteriously suspended for the time being, put on hold, others say."

"And Fremont could continue to maintain his command?"

"Temporarily, yes. The trouble with Fremont is he's more like a playboy. He loves being a general and everything about it. He thrives on the ceremony and all the rituals that are part of the role."

"I have some apple pie for dessert, if you have room, Bert."

"Thanks. I'll take a generous slice."

"From what you say it sounds like Fremont knows little about the priorities of running a war," said Jenny.

"I think that was one of the objections to his command and how it's being conducted."

"Did the secretary decide who was Fremont's successor?"

"Second in command. Jenny, you're an excellent cook. That was a very delicious meal. What are we doing for entertainment now?"

"I have to go to the office to finish my column."

"So late?"

"It's only past noon. I want to get my story in before the evening issue rolls off the press."

"What are you writing about today?"

"Two ladies from Virginia had disguised themselves as country women. They drove a buckboard to D.C. loaded with some antiques, sold them, and with the money they bought things they needed, like green vegetables, shoes, needles and thread, bolts of material, and so on. However, they were stopped at the border on their return to Virginia by Federals. But the Union soldiers felt so sorry for them, they let them pass through."

"Well, I'm not going to spend my time in an empty house," said Bert, rising from the table.

"I wouldn't expect you to."

"Then, let's go."

"Are you going into D.C., too, Bert?"

"Might as well."

* * * *

Jenny was lingering over a cup of coffee the next morning when pounding on the door accompanied by the barks of Mon Vieux disturbed the little quiet she was drinking in.

She opened the door to Bert.

"You again," she said. "Are you here for another meal?"

Bert pushed himself into the house and thrust a copy of yesterday's *Evening Star* on her.

"Read this," he ordered.

She glanced at Personne's column.

"Oh that - about Fremont?"

"Out loud, please," Bert said.

"Is this absolutely necessary, Bert?"

"Yes. Now read."

"Looks like General Fremont is on the way out. A very reliable source reports to me that when Secretary Cameron left for a tour of the Western military departments, he had in his pocket a sealed order to General Fremont to surrender his command post at once.

"There was a lot of saber rattling and Secretary Cameron rode off into the sunset with Fremont. When they returned, Fremont announced he persuaded Secretary Cameron to put the order on the back burner for awhile. But in his heart, Fremont realizes his days of glory are over."

"Stop. That's enough," ordered Bert. "I wonder where that guy Personne got his story. That was going to be my exclusive."

"Simmer down, Bert. What are you going to do about it? Challenge Personne to a duel?"

"Maybe not a duel. I'd like to knock his block off."

"Bert, grow up."

"Do you understand what's at stake here?"

"What?"

"This was my scoop."

"Come off it, Bert. You don't own the news. Ever hear of the freedom of the press?"

"Somebody leaked that story to other members of the press."

"What are you complaining about? Your story is in the *Herald*, isn't it?"

"Yeah, today, not yesterday."

"So?"

"The *Evening Star* beat me to the punch. And when I have a story, I like to think it's exclusive. Nobody else has it."

"Well, it's still exclusive among New York newspapers," said Jenny.

"It's like sharing a byline," Bert said.

"Stop being so melodramatic."

"Who is that guy Personne anyway?"

"I don't know."

"You don't know? How can that be? He's on the staff of your paper, isn't he?"

"His identity is a secret. No one knows who he really is except Mr. Wallach, our editor."

"That's not really playing the game according to the rules, you know - hiding behind anonymity. He can write anything he wants without any fear of recrimination."

"That's the idea that the editor had in mind, I think, to shake up the public with information they'd normally not read because reporters use the regular channels for obtaining information. Even the *New York Times* is saying that if the government is going to hand out secret information, it belongs to all of us."

"Where did Personne get his information?"

"How should I know? Maybe he was on the train with Secretary Cameron. You probably rubbed elbows with him and didn't even know it. You were there, weren't you?"

"Yeah, that's why I thought it was a great story. Cameron had selected only a few of us to be with him."

"Did you know everyone there who had been invited by the Secretary to accompany him?"

"I thought I did. There were a couple of strange faces aboard, but no one introduced me."

"There you are!"

"I'm sure I didn't see him."

"Bert, get with it. How do you know? You wouldn't know him if you saw him anyway."

"What are you so happy about?"

"Isn't that the name of the game: scooping everybody else? Or do the rules change when they suddenly hit you?"

"That's an unfair charge."

"Really? You once said that what counts is the scoop. Nothing else matters, including ethics. You forgot how you praised your friend Carmichael for digging for stories above and beyond the call of duty and respectablility and out scooping everybody."

"But this Fremont story is different," Bert said.

"Why? Because someone got the jump on you this time? It seems to me," said Jenny, "that Mr. Personne is playing fair and square, by the rules. Besides, that's what sells newspapers - the exposé, the inside story of the news. I'm sure you know that already."

"The only person whom I told the story to was you because I knew this wasn't the kind of story you write for your column. You write about -"

"Yeah, corset stays, I know. Don't tell me."

"And you didn't repeat this story to anyone, did you?"

"Why would I, when you had taken me into your very confidence?"

"So how did this guy get the scoop?"

"He was probably on the train with you, as I said before."

"I suppose. Maybe you're right. What annoys me, of course, is the fact that the guy can stay in Washington to file his story, but by the time I get to the telegraph office to file mine, and there's always a line, the Fremont story is already history."

"Bert, don't forget the *Herald* was still the first paper in New York to break the story. That should give you some comfort."

"Small as it is. I'll be back because I don't think this is the end of it."

"Stop whining and don't slam the door when you leave."
Jenny smiled to herself. "All's fair in love and war, Mr. Wells."

* * * *

The doorbell, followed by three rapid-fire knocks, heralded Michel's entrance.

"Thank you for ringing the doorbell," Jenny said.

"You should keep your door locked, cherie. It doesn't make much sense to ask me to ring the doorbell when your door is unlocked."

"I thought you had an undercover assignment."

"I did, but came back late yesterday, and picked up a copy of the *Evening Star*, your paper."

"Michel, you sound upset."

"I have a right to be. Do you know Personne who's on the staff of your paper?"

"No one on the staff knows the true identity except the editor."

"Did you read the column yesterday?" Michel asked.

"Yes, it was about General Fremont, if I recall."

"The bulk of it was, yes; but the last paragraph caught my attention. I get the feeling that the sheriff is waiting to close in on the killer."

"I don't know where you got that impression."

"Chérie, how do you interpret this?" Michel asked.

"The sheriff has collected tangible evidence that will lead to the identity of the killer of Todd, the deserter, and eventually to the arrest and conviction of the murderer."

Michel looked at Jenny, a frown wrinkled his face. "I don't understand. What is tangible evidence?" he asked.

"Do you know what concrete means?"

"Mais non."

"Something solid, something substantial, definite."

"What I just read - what does that mean to you?" Michel asked.

"That sounds to me that the case is an ongoing investigation, but nothing has been resolved as yet."

"Ma chére, I worry that this columnist is placing you in a great danger."

"How?"

"The killer could read this and decide he's going to get rid of you."

"Oh, Michel, but why?"

"If he thinks you'd be able to identify him in any way, he'll kill you."

"First of all, I can't identify the killer because I never saw his face," said Jenny, "and then my memory is a blur."

"But the murderer doesn't know that."

"Michel, how do you know how the killer feels and what he thinks?"

"I don't, I'm just guessing."

"Please don't guess any more; you frighten me."

"Chérie, I don't want to frighten you. But I want you to talk to Personne or talk to the editor, since you don't know who Personne is, and tell him to stop writing about you at once."

"I can't do that. This is Personne's livelihood."

"Chérie, look - he can write about anything he wants to on any topic, like General Fremont, but not about you and the murder case."

"Why are you so insistent about this?"

"Because you're going to get hurt, mark my words. How and where does he get this information anyhow?"

"He knows of my attack. Everyone on the staff knows that. It's common knowledge."

"It's probably a good thing that the identity of Personne is unknown."

"Why?"

"The killer would undoubtedly go after him."

"To do what?"

"Eliminate him. To stop him from writing this tripe."

"Michel, you're getting overly excited about nothing. That wouldn't solve anything."

"Oh yes, it would, by killing him."

She scrutinized him. Is this Michel, the gentleman with the impeccable manners, or is this really a cold-blooded killer? He caught her eye and a smile slithered across his face.

"Don't misunderstand me, chérie. I'm thinking of you, your welfare - nothing more. I don't plan murders. But you need protection from the consequences of the events that this guy will stir up."

"I want you to be alert. I wouldn't want anything to happen to you. You're sure you want me to take Mon Vieux back?"

"Yes. I'm sure I'll be safe."

"Goodbye for now, chérie; take care." He reached for her. She backed away.

"Don't I even rate a hug before I go?"

"No."

"Are you angry with me, chérie?"

"I don't know."

Was his overly solicitous care much too impassioned and only added to her discomfort? Was her imagination stretching beyond belief? It was the same kind of niggling bother that troubled her after the Beauregard interview.

Imagine something that wasn't there? Could she be that foolish? The sheriff told her that there was nothing that could be pinned on Michel. His alibi for September 24th, okayed by Edwin Booth, checked out. She had to accept that.

She walked him to the door. "I'm sorry, Michel - of course I'll give you a hug."

"That's better, chérie. For a minute, I thought you were going to tell me to leave and never come back."

"No. It's just that events have become so overwhelming."

"I understand. I'll drop by tomorrow to see how you are." He kissed her hand. "Au revoir."

It was early afternoon when hoofbeats outside brought Bert to the door. "I just read that Personne column," he said. "Did you see it?"

"You mean today's paper? Oh yeah."

"This guy spells trouble, Jenny."

"What are you talking about?"

"He's setting you up. He talks about the role that a diamond bracelet plays in the murder."

"I know about it. I read the column."

"Do you have a diamond bracelet?"

"Yes."

"You never told me."

"I know I didn't."

"Who gave it to you?"

"Michel."

"That's the way it goes," Bert sighed. "Can I see it?"

"If you want to."

"Yes, I do."

"It's upstairs in my bedroom. I'll go get it."

"Can I come up?"

"No." She walked slowly up the stairs. Why is Bert interested in the bracelet? It has nothing to do with him.

"Here it is. What do you think of it," Jenny asked.

Bert whistled. "Some chunk of ice. Why did Michel give this to you?"

"He asked me to marry him."

"Oh. What was your answer?"

"Bert, don't look so wounded. No."

"Good. Now I can ask you. Will you marry me?"

"No. Certainly not now."

"Then there's still hope for me. And you don't think Personne has you targeted for a murderer's revenge?"

"No. Can't be."

"You know what I think, Jenny?"

"What?"

"That Personne is the real murderer."

Jenny burst out laughing and couldn't stop, as the tears rolled down her face. When she finally gained control, she began to hiccup.

"Jenny, what's the matter with you? Your life may be at stake and all you can do is laugh."

"Personne is not the murderer, I'm sure."

"How do you know if you don't know him."

"First and foremost, he's a journalist. He wants to solve the crime and has taken it on as a kind of crusade."

"That's your story and you're stuck with it. This guy will muddy the waters and put you in danger, besides."

"I don't see it that way."

"Maybe you should. Where does he get all of his information? You told me that no one knows who the real Personne is."

"Anyone with information for this column gives it to the editor who, in turn, passes it on to Personne."

"Then are you telling me you have been spreading the news?"

"I didn't have to. Everyone on the staff knows about my attack. It's common knowledge and so are the particulars of the case."

"And the diamond bracelet? Where did Personne hear about that?"

"He didn't. I wore it to work one day to show it to my friends and somehow or other, it got back to him."

"But why does he make a connection of the bracelet with the murder?"

"I don't know."

"This was not the time to get rid of that dog so fast."

"I thought you told me you were sick of it."

"Maybe it's because it made me think of Michel. But, listen, I worry about you, all alone in this house."

"Why, Bert, you do care."

"Of course, I care, you silly girl. I wouldn't want anything to happen to you. Are you going to be home the rest of the evening?"

"Yes."

"Don't forget to check out all the doors and windows and make sure they're locked."

"I will."

Thirty minutes after Bert had left, Laura stopped by. Jenny was in the back of the house, ready to lock the kitchen door, when the doorbell rang. She ran to the front of the house and greeted her.

"Jenny, don't do anything foolish."

"Such as?"

"Trying to solve Todd's murder by yourself. Big mistake; you can get hurt. The sheriff is experienced and knows what has to be done."

"I don't see that at all. If I work through the Personne column, no one will know that I'm that writer, but maybe I had given the details to the editor and he, on to Personne."

"But think! The killer knows you know about the bracelet from the past."

"I doubt that. There's no accusation in the column and it could mean anything."

"Jenny, talk to the sheriff, I beg of you. Do you think Michel is your assailant?"

"No. Couldn't be."

"So how come he had the bracelet?"

"He told me he bought it in a pawn shop in New York. The killer probably wanted to get rid of the evidence so he could still maintain his anonymity."

"Where's the bracelet now?"

"Upstairs in my dresser. Come on up, I'll let you take another look."

Laura giggled. She held it in her hand. "Jenny, this is a truly beautiful piece of jewelry. Really exquisite."

"Michel told me he thought he could scratch out the inscription, but then he realized he'd deface the bracelet and so left it alone."

"Where are you going to keep it?"

"I think it will be safe in the drawer right here."

Laura looked at her watch. "I better go - Mother is planning an early dinner. Take care of yourself, Jenny."

Jenny walked Laura out to her horse and the girls waved to each other as Laura galloped away.

Jenny returned to the house and decided to continue where she had left off. She knew the kitchen door was still unlocked. First she decided to check the window in the parlor.

A square mirror framed in scrolled rosewood occupied the farther wall of the room. The window was adjacent to the mirror. Jenny automatically glanced at the mirror.

Something flickered and whirred in a flash of color. An insect? Across the mirror. What was it? She froze on the spot. Nothing in this room had budged. She looked at the Ming vase in the corner. Everything was as before. She couldn't move. Someone had just looked in on her. That's what happened. Must have been.

Whoever it was had entered the house through the unlocked kitchen door. She pricked up her ears to listen for footsteps.

If only Laura had stayed a few minutes longer! Her heart pounded. If that had been an insect, it wouldn't have suddenly disappeared like that. She would have heard a buzzing, and the insect would still be in the same room.

She tiptoed out into the hall and reeled when she saw the boots - Hessian tasseled boots underneath the table where she'd place her mail. Her hands trembled. She didn't have any control over them.

Whoever he is, he's upstairs in his stockinged feet. Aunt Irene's gun was also upstairs. Those boots! She shivered. The tassels make them recognizable. She swooned a little, leaned against the wall for support.

Then she remembered. Once again, the recurring nightmare played its course. She saw the Jessie Scout stalk her that night. He came near, hovered over her, hiked up his trousers as he hunkered down and got closer to strike her. On his feet were the Hessian tasseled boots. He's upstairs now - the murderer is upstairs!

She didn't think; she couldn't think! All she knew was that she was beginning to shake and her hands refused to remain still. She did the only thing she could think of at the moment - she fled. She ran out the front door to the barn, saddled her horse, and couldn't urge it fast enough.

By the time she arrived at Laura's house, she had calmed down somewhat. Mrs. Martin answered the door. "Jenny, what's the matter? You look like you've seen a ghost!"

"Maybe I have. Is Laura around?"

"Come in, come, my dear, and tell us what has happened."

Just then Sheriff MacKenzie rode up. "Jennifer, I want to talk to you. Have you read the Personne column for today?"

"No, not yet."

"Let me read the last line to you: 'A reliable source thinks there is a connection between a diamond bracelet with the inscription of 'To A.T. from R.T.' and the murderer.' Are you withholding evidence from me, Jennifer?"

"No."

"So how come I don't have access to this connection to the murderer, but Personne does?"

"I'll make it brief so you can go on your way, Sheriff."

"I'm not going anywhere. I was on my way to see you, then I saw you here at the Martin house. I think it's time, Jennifer, for the truth, the whole truth, and nothing but the truth."

"Sheriff, don't you believe any of the facts I've given you?"

"Oh sure, I believe you, but you've been feeding them to me bit by bit."

"What do you mean, Sheriff?"

"Jennifer, it's time to come clean once and for all."

"I can only tell you what I know, and that's not too much."

"You let me be the judge of that. What you don't understand is that I've got to explore all possibilities. If I think something is strange, off the wall, not quite what is supposed to be normal, I need to ask questions, don't I?"

"Yes."

"All right, let's have it. All of it. Now."

"Years ago, my Aunt Irene was dating an actor in New York who gave her a diamond bracelet with the inscription given in Personne's column. When she asked the actor about the initials, he had, unbeknownst to my aunt, a trumped-up story about the jewelry having been in the family and now they've passed on and he wanted to give it to her.

"Over the passage of time, this actor swindled my aunt out of hundreds of dollars. My aunt returned to D.C.. Some time later, there appeared an ad in the Personal Column of the *Evening Star* by someone inquiring about this self-same bracelet with that inscription.

"My aunt returned the bracelet to its rightful owner and the next thing we heard was that the lady had been murdered and the bracelet was missing."

"Excuse me for interrupting, Jennifer, but was that lady Alice Tiernan?"

"Yes, it was."

"That case was never solved."

"Well, to bring you up to the present, Michel Dubonnet presented me with the very same bracelet with that very inscription in it as a gift."

"Where did he get it?"

"He bought it in a pawn shop in New York. At least, that's what he told me."

"What are you doing here at the Martin house anyway?"

"Sheriff, I'm ashamed to say I fled from my house."

"Why?"

"Someone had entered the house and was sneaking around in his stockinged feet. I was so frightened, I couldn't leave the house fast enough."

"I thought you had a gun."

"I do, but it's in my bedroom."

"Do you know what he was after?"

"No."

"Let's ride back to your home and see if he took anything of value."

"Let me tell the Martins I'll be back."

Both Laura and her mother were waiting on the porch.

"What's all the excitement about?" asked Laura.

"I'll tell you all about it when I return. The sheriff wants to accompany me home."

As they rode together, the sheriff said, "I came over to tell you to be careful, Jennifer."

"Careful about what?"

"That guy who writes that Personne column is no friend of yours."

"Why do you say that?"

"I believe there's a veiled threat to your life in it."

"I didn't get that impression."

"He talks about a link with the murderer. Who are all these reliable but anonymous sources feeding him information? That wouldn't be you, would it, Jennifer?"

"I told you I don't know who Personne is, only my editor does."

"Don't you see him when he comes to the office?" the sheriff asked.

"He has his own office and the door is always closed."

"But he still has to come to work in the morning, doesn't he?"

"No, he works at night when no one is around. Our editor mentioned to me if I wanted to give out any information, write it briefly, place it on his desk, and he'd find it when he'd come to work at night."

"I think his statements and insinuations will make someone out there mighty nervous."

"Good - don't nervous people make mistakes?" asked Jenny.

"Maybe. But nervous people can also be dangerous. For a guy who hangs around the office only at night, Personne seems to have a lot of background information about you, the attack, and the subsequent loss of memory."

"Just about everyone on the staff knows about that."

"And what about the bracelet?"

"I wore it to work one day to show friends. There was nothing secretive about it."

"Why does Personne link the bracelet with the murder?"

"I don't know."

"Another amateur detective busily at work. He's going to interfere with my own investigation. You should talk to the editor and tell him to tell Personne to lay off. Not tell him, order him to do so, to stop writing about the murder case because he's putting you in grave danger."

"I thought that helped our cause by flushing out the assassin wherever and whoever he is."

"Not the way I see it, Jennifer. Don't forget this man is a killer. He has already murdered two people, perhaps more we don't know about, and who knows what's going on in his head when he reads this column."

"Maybe he isn't even in the area."

"If he's over the border into Virginia, he reads the EVENING STAR. Remember, I'm the only one who is authorized to investigate this case and who has the experience to do so. Neither the newspaper or Personne has either.

"Jennifer, look over there. Your barn door is open."

"Sheriff, I didn't lock it. I just fled. I was very frightened."

"O.K., let's go inside and see what has been taken, if anything. Your front door is unlocked, too. Did you know that?"

"Yes, I just bolted and ran without rhyme or reason. You'll find the kitchen door in the rear, too, also unlocked."

"You certainly made it easy for this guy to enter your home."

Nothing seemed to be out of place on the first floor.

"Everything just the way you left it?" the sheriff asked. "Then let's go upstairs."

Jenny knew immediately what to look for: the diamond bracelet in her dresser drawer - gone!

"Looks like your murderer is in the area," the sheriff said, "and he reads the Personne column."

"I'll ride back with you, Sheriff; I want to stop at Laura's."

"Did you lock everything up, Jennifer?"

"Yes."

"Doors and windows?"

"Yes."

"Jennifer, I hope you understand why I don't want any interference with my investigation."

"Yes."

"That's why it's very important that any information is funneled directly to me."

"I'll do my best to see you get everything."

"I'll hold you to that, Jennifer. Oh, by the way, I read your interview with General Beauregard."

"And?"

"I found it interesting, but I wondered how you wangled an appointment with him?"

"Connections, Sheriff, connections."

The sheriff laughed. "Is this the part where I'm supposed to give you the third degree?"

"I hope not."

* * * *

"I thought you'd never get back," Laura said. "I've been sitting on pins and needles. Tell us what happened."

"What happened was while I was locking a window in the parlor, someone entered the house through the kitchen door."

"Jenny, didn't you lock that door?" asked Mrs. Martin.

"I hadn't gotten around to it at that time."

"So - after the intruder entered the house through the kitchen door," Mrs. Martin said, "what happened next? Did you see him?"

"No. He had removed his boots and had gone upstairs."

"Where were you?" asked Laura.

"I was still in the parlor, locking a window. I hadn't heard him because he was walking in his stockinged feet. When I walked out into the hall to go into the kitchen to lock that back door, I saw the boots - Hessian tasseled, Laura, like we saw at Reynolds' Bootery."

"What did you do?" Laura asked.

"My memory picked up on the attack and vividly played it out for me as before. I wonder when that nightmare will end."

"When did this all happen?" asked Laura.

"It was just a few minutes after you had visited me."

"If only I had known."

"Jenny, what did you do?" asked Mrs. Martin.

"I fled. That's why I appeared suddenly on your doorstep."

"The murderer," said Laura, "he was still upstairs then?"

"Yes. I could never have faced him. I was much too much frightened."

"When you and the sheriff returned to your home, what did you find missing?" asked Mrs. Martin.

"The diamond bracelet - nothing else."

A day later Laura dropped over to visit. "Jenny, have you seen Michel?"

"No. As a matter of fact, he said he was going to come yesterday to see how I was. He never showed. It's unusual for him to make a promise and not follow through. Maybe he was called away unexpectedly for an intelligence mission."

"Well, I saw him yesterday."

"You're sure you didn't mistake him for someone else?"

"No."

"Where did you see him? What was he doing?"

"I had gone downtown shopping and he had the buckboard and had come out of O'Malley's Bakery, carrying pies, loading them in the wagon."

"Did you speak to him?"

"Yes. I said, 'Hello, Michel. How are you?'
He looked directly at me, no sign of recognition on his face, as he continued to stare at me. No smile, nothing. He wasn't the happy Frenchman you know."

"I had a feeling something had happened," Jenny said, "but I didn't know what."

"So you don't know how he felt about Personne's column and the diamond bracelet?"

"I wondered what his reaction would be to that."

"I think you've already seen his response," said Laura. "He's going to ignore you. He's angry."

"I knew he'd be upset about what he read."

"But what's with the pies?" asked Laura.

"Oh, that! He had told me one way he's able to move freely in and out of Southern lines is to pose as a sutler, selling pies and cakes to the men. He said he picks up a lot of information that way."

"Did the sheriff ever question Michel as to where he was the night of September 24th?" Laura asked.

"Yes. Michel had a good airtight alibi."

"What could possibly be that airtight?"

"He was on the stage at Grover's Theater, in the role of the Duke of Clarence in *Richard 111*."

"Anybody confirm this?"

"Yes, the sheriff told me he had written to Edwin Booth who verified Michel's story. Booth had the lead in the play."

"Are you going to contact Michel and find out what's bothering him?"

"No," said Jenny. "He knows where I live if he wants to see me."

"You know, Jenny, there was something furtive the way Michel was stacking those pies in the wagon."

"What do you mean?"

"As if he didn't want anyone to see what he was doing and as if he were in a terrific hurry to get away, to flee."

"You're sure about that?"

"He kept turning his head and looking in different directions. Then he would dash back into the bakery, get some more boxes of pies, store them in the wagon, all the time turning his head, searching, looking around. That's how I spotted him. All that activity made me focus on him. If he were trying to be inconspicuous, he would have been unobserved if his activity hadn't been so frenetic".

"Jenny, maybe it's worth your while to see the sheriff and tell him about Michel's strange behavior."

"I'll see."

"Maybe the sheriff could have a deputy follow him around to see what he's up to."

"Laura, come into the library with me."

"What are you going to do?" Laura asked.

"I think its time for me to re-read this."

"What?"

Jenny showed her the book.

"Shakespeare? Why now in the middle of everything?"

"I think that *Richard 111* might offer a clue."

"How?"

"As yet, I don't know. Besides, it'll be good for my soul."

"Well, I'll run along."

Two hours later Jenny took her volume of Shakespeare and went to see the sheriff.

"Got a minute?" she asked, poking her head into his office.

"If you have a clue, you bet," Sheriff MacKenzie said.

"Maybe bigger than I can handle."

"Congratulations for finally coming to me for help."

"Sheriff, ever read Shakespeare?"

"Yeah, in school - *Julius Caesar, Macbeth, Hamlet.*"

"What about *Richard 111*?"

"Let's see. Is that the one that goes, 'A horse, a horse, my kingdom for a horse?'"

Jenny laughed. "That's it."

"Outside of that one line, I don't remember too much about the play. There were a couple of murders in it, I think."

"I'll loan you my copy so you can review it." She extended the book to him.

"Jennifer, wait - I appreciate your desire to educate me, but at the moment it's just not relevant to what I'm doing."

"Meaning?"

"The murder case."

"Oh, but it is. Read *Richard 111* and learn about the Duke of Clarence."

"That's the role Michel played, isn't it?"

"That's right."

"Can't you tell me what you read?"

"Sheriff, if you don't have time to read the entire play, read Act I and I guarantee you'll have your suspect."

"This is about as bad as withholding evidence from me, Jennifer." He laughed.

"Sheriff, you once told me that if you suspected someone, you'd ask yourself whether the suspect had the opportunity to commit the murder."

"Yes, that's right."

"On that basis, you concluded that Michel, for instance, did not have the opportunity to kill Todd."

"He had an ironclad alibi and the endorsements of Edwin Booth - that he was there at the theater in *Richard 111* in the role of the Duke of Clarence and he was quite visible during the curtain calls. Therefore, how could he possibly be at the murder scene September 24th?"

"But if you read *Richard 111*, you'd discover that the Duke of Clarence is murdered in Act I Scene iv and is no longer seen in the play."

"So what you're saying, Jennifer, is he'd have a chance to leave the theater, stop at his home to change his clothes, run up to Martha's, kill Todd, then return to his house, get back in costume, and appear at the theater where he slipped in without raising any suspicion and could take his curtain calls. Very clever."

"I recall that when the murderer was stalking me," Jenny said," he asked, 'Where's Todd?' He wanted to make sure he was in the right place."

"Jennifer, you've really hit on something."

"It sounds good, plausible, but there's one piece of the puzzle that doesn't fit."

"The fact he was dressed as a Jessie Scout?"

"He could have a uniform at home like that, I suppose, but then again, why would he?"

"What else?"

"I never did see his face because the bandanna concealed it. But Mr. Reynolds of the Bootery described the Jessie Scout who bought the Hessian boots: dark hair, pencil thin moustache, otherwise clean-shaven. There is no facial similarity whatsoever to the man I know as Michel. You know what he looks like, too, Sheriff."

"There's always the possibility that another Jessie Scout had bought the Hessian boots."

"From what Mr. Reynolds told me, I doubt it. The boots are very expensive and the customers that Mr. Reynolds recalled who had bought the boots during this period were doctors, lawyers, and dentists."

"Maybe Michel - assuming he is now an authentic suspect - hired another Jessie Scout to do the killing," said the sheriff.

"Then what would be the point of his having to race home, change clothes, and so on to commit the murder?"

The sheriff laughed. "Jennifer, we're still speculating. This is just a supposition you have and at this point, we don't really know if it's correct. Have you discussed this theory with anyone else? I'm talking about Act I Scene iv?"

"No."

"Then don't, for obvious reasons. In no way do I want Michel to think I'm considering him as a suspect. He could flee and we'd never find him. I want him in the area, so he will be available for arrest, if your theory is proved correct."

"Do you think you're closer to making an arrest now?"

"No, because we have these other problems to straighten out. Also, I should have some kind of tangible evidence, something substantial to hang your conjectures on."

CHAPTER X

Bert was on his way to Jenny's house when Sheriff MacKenzie hailed him.

"Are you headed for Jennifer's?"

"Yes, how did you guess?" Bert asked.

"A little bird told me. I'll save you a trip. She's not at home," the sheriff said. "I need to talk to her."

"We can ride over to Laura's. Maybe she knows," said Bert.

"Before we go," the sheriff said, "could you step into my office for a minute?"

"What's going on, Sheriff?"

"My two deputies are out of town on a case and I need a deputy for a backup. I want to deputize you."

"That's not quite in my field. Wait - I don't know if I want this." Bert held up his hand to ward off anything the sheriff might say.

"Bert, this is just temporary - a one-time deal only."

"It's kind of sudden. I mean, I should think about it."

"I have to have another man to accompany me."

"You're not listening to what I said, Sheriff."

"Oh yes, I am."

"Sheriff, what are you doing?"

"I'm strapping this holstered six shooter around your waist."

"I didn't know I had consented."

"You didn't, but I figured you'd want to help Jennifer."

"Is she in danger?"

"We don't know yet. Have you ever fired a six-shooter?"

"Many times."

"Well, and here I thought you were the reluctant deputy."

"I own one and use it in target practice."

"That's a break for me."

"Now that we got that out of the way," Bert said, "where are we going?"

"I have a search warrant to enter Michel Dubonnet's house."

"What's that all about?"

"Let's say, I have a gut feeling about that guy," the sheriff said.

"You can't get a search warrant based purely on a gut feeling, can you, Sheriff?"

"You're right, but I think I can build a pretty good case against Michel."

"What did he do?"

"Committed a murder, maybe a couple."

"I wish Jenny were around to hear this."

They entered the house and began their search. Bert found himself drawn immediately to the picture of Edwin Booth. The sheriff moved with single-mindedness, directing his path to the bedroom. He pawed through the clothes in the closet and called out to Bert.

"Come here - look at this! A regular costume shop!"

The closet disclosed all kinds of uniforms: Zouave, three Confederate jackets but one pair of grey trousers, one pair of Union pants, and one Union overcoat.

"Here's a priest's cassock with the dog collar on a hanger," said Bert. "Wonder what he did with this? What kind of business was Michel in?"

"The business of disguise," said the sheriff.

"Whose?"

"His. The Confederate jackets were part of the Jessie Scout uniform, but see this jacket, Bert?"

"A button's missing."

"That's right and I have that button, I'm sure. The night Jenny was attacked, she had been standing to the side, then dropped to the ground when the assailant fired and killed the deserter.

"Then she stood up, but the attacker stalked her, pushed her down, and she tried to push him back as he hovered over her. When she pushed him back, her fingers wrapped around a button on his jacket. He slammed into her and she fell, pulling the button off at the same time.

"The button was found in her hand when I brought her to the hospital. I saved that button and I bet it fits the configuration here with its missing threads.

"Bert, how about going through the dresser drawers while I finish up my search in the closet?"

"Sheriff, here in the corner, all these toupees, different styles, different colors. And look what I found in the top drawer: is this the infamous diamond bracelet I've heard about?"

"Give it to me," the sheriff said. He flipped it over.
"There's the same inscription: 'To A.T. from R.T.'. The evidence is piling up. Did you look through the rest of the drawers?"

"Yes. Only personal things like socks, underwear, cuff links."

"Bert, I don't think you know, but Jennifer's house was burglarized."

"Again? When?"

"Yesterday, in the daytime."

"I just visited Jenny to tell her to be sure to lock up then."

"That's what she was doing when the burglar entered the house through the unlocked back door in the kitchen."

"He didn't hurt her, did he?"

"No. When Jennifer walked into the hall and saw a pair of Hessian boots there, she panicked and fled. This bracelet was stolen from Jennifer's house.

"The A.T. on this bracelet was a lady named Alice Tiernan, the original owner of it. She was murdered, but we never found her killer."

"O.K., so we find the bracelet in Michel's house, but how do you know Michel is tied up with that murder?"

"We don't as yet. There are a few missing links. That bracelet had been given to Jennifer's aunt by a certain Len Castle. Remember that photo of the aunt and her actor friend Len Castle that was taken in an earlier burglary?"

"I never saw the picture, but Jenny told me about it."

"That diamond bracelet was given to Jennifer's aunt as a gift and it had the same inscription on it, so we know we are talking about the same bracelet."

"How did it get back to Alice Tiernan?" Bert asked.

"She had advertised in the Personal column. Jennifer's aunt answered the ad, returned the bracelet, and then Alice Tiernan was murdered later and the bracelet was stolen."

"But Len Castle isn't Michel Dubonnet, is he?" asked Bert.

"That's what I mean. We have quite a few things to clear up yet before we can put the cuffs on Michel.

"I think it's time for us to head over to Laura's," the sheriff said, "and see if she knows where Jennifer is. First, I'll make a quick stop at the office and put this bracelet in the safe."

Laura was surprised to see the men and ushered them into her house. "Yes, Jenny had stopped by."

"How long ago?" the sheriff asked.

"I don't know. Maybe an hour ago, not more than that. Is she in danger?"

"If we can get to her in time, no."

"She told me Michel wanted to see her and it was urgent. She thought maybe he was ill."

"Yeah, he's ill, all right," the sheriff said. "Where are they meeting, do you know?"

"There's a little copse of trees about a half mile or so from her home. We used to picnic there. There's a meandering creek nearby. Does that help?"

"We'll find it."

* * * *

Jenny was in her kitchen, lingering over her coffee, and thinking of what her column should deal with and then Personne's column. She smiled. She enjoyed playing the role of a phantom columnist and still keep her identity under wraps.

Her reverie was broken by two loud thumps on the front door, as if someone had thrown something. She approached the door timidly and opened it. For a minute, she thought of Michel. The man before her was dressed as a Zouave, but he wasn't Michel. He was short and stocky.

"Pardon, mademoiselle, I have a note to bring you."

"From whom?" Jenny was afraid to touch the note.

"Michel."

"Are you a friend of his?"

"You could say that."

"Well, thank you. Do I have to give you an answer?"

"No. The note will explain everything. Au revoir."

Jenny closed the door and sat down to read and study the message: "I need you, chérie. This is urgent. Meet me at our usual place by the creek. Hurry."

Jenny dressed quickly and rode over to Laura's. "Laura, what do you think of it?" she asked when Laura finished reading the note.

"I wonder if this might be a trap."

"Laura, how could that be? You're thinking about my Personne column? There's no way Michel could ever identify me as Personne."

"I don't know, but I'm wary the way that note was delivered to you by that Zouave."

"I think something happened to Michel. Maybe he's ill."

"Then why didn't he say so in the note?"

"You know, he hasn't been around for a few days."

"Ever since you wrote that the diamond bracelet was linked to a murder."

"I'm going to meet him."

"You're sure you're making the right decision?"

"There's nothing menacing in his message."

"Why don't you notify the sheriff, Jenny, before you go?"

"And then what? He'll show up at the head of a posse and when he finds us, we'll be sitting and talking."

"Isn't it peculiar, Jenny, Michel wants to meet you secretly?"

"I suppose the column bothered him."

"Jenny, that doesn't excuse him. He doesn't have an inkling you are Personne."

"True."

"So if you're such great friends, he'd come and talk to you about his problem, wouldn't he?"

"Perhaps."

"Jenny, didn't he drop in to see you when he was troubled by the words 'tangible evidence' in a previous column?"

"Yes, he did. Maybe he's not well."

"You're just trying to find a legitimate reason why he hasn't showed."

"I have to, even though there are some unexplainable instances tied up with Michel that defy a reasonable answer."

"You're not serious about him, are you, Jenny?"

"No. Nothing like that."

"If Michel were innocent, really innocent of any wrongdoing, I can see," Laura said, "he would come to you if he had something to say, something bothering him."

"Of course, unless he's ill."

"You want to give him the benefit of the doubt. But suppose he were guilty...."

"Guilty of what?"

"Murder, Jenny. You know that as well as I."

"Yes. There are details that are questionable about his behavior, but still nothing that the sheriff can nail down specifically."

"Why?"

"Too many holes in the theory. Without any tangible evidence, the sheriff told me he can do nothing."

"I hope I'm mistaken, Jenny, but I find this note sinister. So what are you going to do?"

"I'm going to meet with him. He asked me to come to see him and I will."

"Want me to go with you?"

"That won't be necessary. I'll talk to you when I get back," Jenny said. An hour later, Jenny arrived at the rendezvous. She dismounted, tethered her horse to one of the trees, and began to walk. There was no sign of Michel anywhere. Was this a hoax, but for what ulterior motive? She didn't know.

She began calling, "Michel, where are you? Michel, can you hear me?"

"I'm over here, Jenny, this way. Stop - look to the left."

Before her, stood Michel, dressed in Confederate grey with a white kerchief spread over his shoulder with the end hanging down.

"Michel?" Jenny asked.

"Yes, Jenny - it's me."

"But why are you wearing that uniform?"

She didn't hear what he said. Instead she stood mesmerized as the image triggered her nightmare all over again. Once more she saw another Confederate dressed as a Jessie Scout, walking towards her, a rifle in his hand. She placed her hands over her ears, as he fired. Then he moved to her, striking her with his fist. She fell, and he hovered over her, hitting her again.

She looked down at his boots, the tasseled Hessian boots. He was down on his haunches and whacked her. Will she ever exorcise it from her memory. It had all come back to her as if it were happening in the present.

Michel ran over to her as she lay on the ground. "Let me help you up,

Jenny." He was wearing the Hessian tasseled boots.

"Don't touch me."

"Jenny, are you all right? Speak to me!"

"Stay away from me! Don't hit me!"

"Jenny, it's me Michel - I'm not going to hit you."

"You're a Jessie Scout. But you're Michel, aren't you?"

"Jenny, get up. Here, let me help you."

Is this occurring now or is this part of the past? The location, the place - where is it? Had she been there then, before, long ago? Her memory was playing games with her. She was disoriented and tried to get her bearings, to keep her memory focused in the present.

"Jenny, stand up. please," Michel said. "Look at me - you recognize me." He rolled the white kerchief into a ball and threw at her. "Here's another signature of mine." He removed his toupee.

"Are you a spy for the South?" she finally asked.

"One of the finest performances of my life. A pity I couldn't play to a full house instead of on a one-on-one basis." He pulled off the side whiskers from his face as he spoke. "Are you good at keeping secrets?"

"Of course." She retreated a little.

"I was never a real Jessie Scout, but the role was too good to pass up. Stay here! Don't leave, my love."

"Don't call me that. You killed Todd, didn't you?"

"Now how could I do that when I was taking curtain calls?" He pulled off his moustache.

"Easily. Oh sure, you were taking curtain calls, all right, but the role of Duke of Clarence ends Act I Scene iv because he is murdered then and he's no longer needed in the play."

"I always knew I'd be proud of you, chérie. Go to the head of the class."

"And because the play goes for a bit longer, you had lots of time to go home, change into the Confederate uniform with the white kerchief, and head up to Todd's house. After the murder, you returned home, changed back into the costume of Duke of Clarence, and reported to the theater in plenty of time to take your curtain calls."

"Bravo, bravo." He applauded.

"Were you a courier for Rose O'Neal Greenhow?"

"Whatever made you think that?"

"That wicked wink General Beauregard gave you when he spoke of Mrs. Greeenhow's courier. You said he owed you a big favor. That was it, wasn't it?"

"Rose and I are on a first name basis. Pity, such a talented woman like that mouldering in a jail, all because the North doesn't know what to do with her. But she's clever. She'll get out. Yes, I was the courier who carried the message about General McDowell. I can remember those famous words that saved the day for the South, as if it were yesterday: 'McDowell's troops intend to destroy the railroad from Winchester to Manassas to prevent the arrival of Johnston's troops.'"

His voice made every word ring like a Shakespearean soliloquy.

"Were you lovers?"

"One love letter to a lady doesn't mean a love affair. No, I had my eyes on you. Couldn't you guess? Didn't you know?"

"Then you struck me because you didn't want me to identify you. Is that right?"

"Right again, my pet." He removed his beard.

"But why did you have to kill Todd?"

"He caught me eavesdropping outside the tent of a Union officer. I had ducked behind the tent when I heard the officer getting ready to leave. After that, I rushed into the tent, grabbed some papers that were on the desk and when I left, this guy Todd was standing there and demanded to know where I was going with the stack of papers in my hand. Imagine! The guy wasn't even an officer! I do not answer to a mere private, thank you! I punched him in the jaw and he fell to the ground like the lightweight he was.

"I made my getaway safely, but I knew then that my work for the South was in jeopardy and I could wind up in prison. There was only one solution: eliminate Todd."

"How did you know where he lived?"

"That was simple. The guy was lying on the ground after I socked him so I found one of the soldiers in his company and asked him to help me move Todd and then asked for Todd's name and where he lived. I left the scene shortly after. Todd was still out for good."

Jenny stared at him. Michel no longer was speaking English with a French accent. "Why are you talking like an American?" she asked.

"Because I am one."

"You wear glasses," she said, as she watched him slip on a pair.

"The better to see you, my love." He bowed. "Len Castle, at your service, mademoiselle."

"Didn't you forget about your limp?" she asked.
"The leg is healed, I suppose."

"That limp was strictly for show. It was one of my better limps, since you remember it so well."

"Why are you revealing yourself now?"

"You're getting too close to me. I didn't like some of the things that Personne character wrote in his column and now's the time to play my hand and get away safely.

"An actor's life is defined by a series of entrances and exits. Did you know that, my love? Very shortly, I will make my last entrance and exit. But this time you're coming with me."

Jenny backed away. "Oh no, I'm not - I can't!"

"Just think, if Personne weren't meddling, we'd still be friends. Who knows, maybe, even more, wouldn't we, chérie? Who appointed him anyhow to solve the murder?

"The biggest mistake I made was to give you that diamond bracelet. It's a beauty, isn't it?"

"Yes."

"That bracelet has caused me more grief than General Beauregard ever caused the North. I wasn't aware you knew the history of that jewelry."

"My aunt told me."

"Ah yes, dear, sweet, glamorous Irene."

"What about the grief you caused Alice Tiernan's family?"

"Yes," he said, "unfortunate. But the problem was I was becoming very fond of you, ma chére, and hoped, in time, we'd become lovers, real lovers. I wanted to give you some token of my affection, something that would bind you to me."

"Surely, you'd know our relationship couldn't or wouldn't go on, that eventually, I'd find out about your spying and your murdering innocent people."

"Yes, how true." He sighed. "I thought that might happen but with the war keeping everyone so busily occupied, I didn't believe that the murder of one miserable deserter would make any headlines. Stay where you are! You're coming with me."

Jenny retreated. "That's what you think. I can't."

"Oh yes, you can and you will, ma chére. He leaned forward and grabbed her. "Stop struggling! How can I let you roam freely when you know all about me?"

Jenny looked down at his boots.

"Admiring my Hessian beauties? As precious as the beauty in my arms."

"You entered my house."

"Why shouldn't I? We were great friends, more than that, weren't we, and I knew my way around."

"How could you?"

"Oh, I know why you're so upset. I didn't ring the doorbell and you didn't want me to just march in, did you?"

She slapped his face.

"Now, now - is that a nice thing to do? I'm sure you understand that I had to reclaim the diamond bracelet."

"You gave it to me."

"My love, when I read Personne's column that the sheriff had some tangible evidence, I knew it wouldn't be long before he would be breathing down my neck. Of course, I had to take the bracelet for my own protection, my own safety." His lips brushed lightly against hers.

"Stop that!"

"Then the next day when I read the column and Personne intimated the link between the bracelet and a murder, I became a little rattled."

She looked at him.

"Yes, my love, even professionals like me get panicky. I was glad the bracelet was in my possession." He planted a kiss on her cheek.

She slapped him again.

"Why are you so physical? I haven't done anything to hurt you. Stop squirming; I'm not going to let you go - I can't. Don't you understand?"

"I'll never forgive you for breaking into my house and frightening me."

"You have a phobia about doorbells, don't you? Because I don't ring them?"

"That didn't frighten me as much as seeing your boots underneath that table in the hall and -"

"Knowing I was walking around upstairs in my stockinged feet?"

"Yes."

"But you understand why I had to do that because if I had worn my boots, you would have heard me. When I entered your house, I didn't even have to break in because the kitchen door was open. That was so thoughtful of you!"

"I never got around to locking it. Did you break into the house before this and steal that picture of you and Aunt Irene?"

"Of course. C'est moi. Who else would it be, but me? I didn't expect to find you home. I had it all planned: I would sneak in, take the photo, sneak out and no one would be the wiser. So I was taken by surprise. You were staying with the Martins and I was sure I could pull off my little caper safely in an empty house."

"I changed my mind the last minute."

"Just like a woman - I should have known! Surely, you must know now why I had to break in."

"You stole that photo!"

"I had to. I couldn't afford to be identified as Len Castle, especially with a murder charge hanging over my head."

"But you had already disguised yourself as Michel Dubonnet. No one would recognize you as Len Castle."

"You never can tell and I wasn't taking any chances."

"What did you do with that picture?"

"What would you do if you found some tangible evidence that might prove incriminating?"

"I'd probably burn it."

"Well said. You were quite amusing when you caught me and my, you acted so grown up with that gun in your hand, protecting the old homestead!"

"You're lucky I didn't shoot you."

"I really didn't think you would. Your answers to my questions and your shaking hand told me more than you realized. You were much too scared to take my life. Anything else you want to know?"

"One thing I couldn't figure out: remember the day Bert, Laura, and I were in a balloon? We had just been launched. We were in the air and there you were running toward us, flailing your arms, yelling at us to return, to land."

"But you didn't return to me."

"Bert didn't want to. We had just gotten in the air, and we couldn't figure out what the urgency was."

"There was an urgency, all right."

"Bert felt that as newspaper reporters we'd be privy to any late breaking story."

"The urgency was that was the day a friend of mine and I had planned to hold up a wagon train coming out of Lynn, Massachusetts with a load of shoes. Something our Southern soldiers needed desperately. You see, I always work for the war effort. We had already committed ourselves to the job and could not change plans."

"You thought, I suppose, I'd see you, recognize you, and blow your cover."

"That's right. Later I realized you wouldn't be able to identify me anyway because I'd be wearing a Jessie Scout uniform and would make a point of having my face partially concealed."

"Michel, why do you participate in crimes like that?"

"I have a question for you: how do you think I could take you to the Willard's for dinner or even breakfast, to say nothing of that magnificent four horse drawn brougham I hired to pick you up? Do you think I could afford those trimmings on an actor's salary?"

"But you had such a fine reputation as an actor! You would jeopardize that for a petty crime?"

"You can't eat reputation. You forget, too, that once a play has run its course, that means the actors are unemployed and if they can't find any more theatrical roles, they have to scrounge around to earn some money."

"You could have upheld your principles and gotten a job as a waiter to tide you over till the next acting part."

"Well, principles, like reputation, gilt-edged words as they are don't bring in the cash. As for your other suggestion - I should be a waiter?"

"There's nothing wrong with honest work," Jenny said.

"My dear, where's your sense of proportion? I'm a Shakespearean actor and waiting on someone is, should I say, beneath me. Completely out of the question."

"Now that it's over..."

"What do you mean 'over'? I expect to get out of here and you're coming with me."

"Do you think it was worth it - robbing and murdering?"

"The murders had nothing to do with these jobs. I had some of the best paying part-time jobs you could ever imagine. Oh yes, I was paid handsomely for the shoes I brought the Confederates. Another benefit of this kind of employment - I could always work it in between acting stints. My acting roles enabled me to keep a low profile so no one ever suspected me, until they would either see the play, maybe, or review it like you."

"Now I want to tell you what you did to me."

"What are you talking about? I never as much as harmed a hair on your head."

"Not like that. But every time I saw a Jessie Scout, my memory would dredge up from the farthest recesses of my brain the nightmare of your killing Todd and then coming after me to strike."

"Sorry about that. I didn't mean to."

"Your apology is unacceptable. I have been through my own private hell while you blithely walked away."

"Now that you know that I'm the culprit, what are you going to do about it?"

"What can I do? I'm virtually your prisoner. Let me go." She struggled against him.

"I have become very fond of you, Jenny, and what I have to do breaks my heart."

"Are you going to kill me?"

"No. I can't stoop to such violence."

"What do you want with me then?"

"You're going to go to la belle France with me and we're going to live happily ever after and no one will ever find us."

"I'm not going with you."

"You have to, now that you know so much about me."

"I can't."

"You will. As soon as I'd free you, you'd run to your dear friend, Sheriff MacKenzie, wouldn't you?"

He groped for the gun in his pocket, still holding her tightly.

"You do carry a gun."

"Only when I have to."

"I thought you don't believe in violence."

"I don't but sometimes a gun is necessary for a little persuasion."

She could only think of the people he had already killed. How will she ever get away now without being a casualty herself?

"You're so subdued, chérie. Nothing more to say? It's a wonder what one little gun can do."

From within the copse, Sheriff MacKenzie's voice boomed, "Let her go, Michel or Len Castle or whatever your name is."

"Speak of the devil," said Michel.

The sheriff had drawn his gun. "Have your gun ready, Bert, but don't shoot as long as he's holding Jennifer."

"You yell to the sheriff that he should leave," Michel said.

She shook her head.

"You will or else." He pushed the gun into her ribs. "Listen to me. You tell the sheriff you've decided to go with me, understand? Now speak."

"Sheriff," Jenny called. She started to cry.

"Control yourself," Michel ordered.

"Jennifer, are you all right?" Sheriff MacKenzie yelled out. "Let me hear from you."

She started to speak again, then cried.

"Answer him, damn you."

"I'm fine, Sheriff," she said, trying to keep her voice from trembling.

Bert glanced at the sheriff. "You hear that? She sounds like she's crying again."

"Sheriff," Jenny began, "I decided to go with Michel, so you can leave."

"Are you sure that's what you want to do, Jennifer?" the sheriff yelled.

"Yes," she struggled to say but a sob caught in her throat.

"Bert, she's in trouble. She's speaking under duress," the sheriff said.

"What can we do?" Bert asked.

"I know Jennifer. She never had any intentions of going with Michel."

"That makes me feel better," Bert said.

"Bert, this is not a time to declare your love! I need your help to rescue Jennifer."

"How are we going to do that?"

"First, we're going to pretend that we accept her statement. Then, I'll say I'm leaving the area, but we'll try to conceal ourselves and look for an opportunity to rescue her." The sheriff cupped his hands over his mouth. "We're leaving, Michel. You can release her."

"Sheriff, I never made any kind of an agreement like that with you.

Jenny stays with me and I'm holding on to her. You heard her - she wants to go with me."

"Well, all right, if that's what Jennifer wants, fine with me. Goodbye."

Silence ensued. Jenny couldn't stanch the flow of tears that spilled over on her cheeks.

"I don't believe the sheriff left," Michel said. "Why are you crying? I haven't hurt you."

"I want to stay in Washington."

"I can't let you do that. I'd have the sheriff and his posse scouring the countryside for me once he gets the description he needs from you."

"Do you think you can face the sheriff and a court of law and a jury later on with the murders you committed?" Jenny started to cry. "Of course," she began, sniffling, "you can always give your best performance as a liar."

Jenny was depressed after hearing the sheriff, her one and only hope for a rescue.

"Well, my love - all your friends have deserted you."

"You'll pay for this!"

"I doubt it."

"Some day I'll testify against you in court and you'll be put away forever. Whatever happens now, I expect to have the last word," said Jenny.

"That's what you think. You're going to marry me and you'll never be able to testify against me as my wife."

"Over my dead body."

"You don't give me much choice, do you?"

She wept copiously. All she wanted was to get away from him as far as possible. She realized the only chance for escape was to catch him off guard. But how? Her mind raced for some solution. He was bigger and stronger; she could never overpower him. Nor could she fool him with any kind of a trick.

"Did you hear something?" he asked. "Came from there, in the underbrush." He turned his head in the direction of the noise and Jenny kicked him in the groin. He doubled over, moaning, and staggered. She pulled her hand free and took off.

She had to get away from him as fast as she could. This could be to her advantage, since she knows the area and he doesn't. She heard him tearing after her. She remembered there was a hill around here somewhere. She didn't know how near it was, but if she got there, it could provide her with a little shelter till the sheriff came back to rescue her. She had to believe he wouldn't abandon her and didn't leave.

She vaguely recalled there was a ravine, too, at the bottom of the hill. Beyond that, a meandering creek framed in the wilderness.

She was already gasping for breath and wondered how much longer she could continue. The fact that he might be in hot pursuit, gave her the adrenalin to push further.

She arrived at the hill and debated where she should hide. The wisps of an early morning fog lingered over the ravine below.

Then Jenny heard a noise. It sounded like someone, Michel probably, with a stick, thrashing and beating through the underbrush, looking for her. Without thinking, she plunged into the thicket, oblivious of the brambles scratching her hands and arms as she flew down the hill into the ravine.

How much time had elapsed since her flight, she didn't know and couldn't tell. She stayed near some shrubs and trees. No longer able to stand on her legs, she sagged against the trunk of the nearest tree till she hit the ground in despair. Keyed up, choked up, stirred up, her energies spent - how will she ever free herself from Michel?

She began to drift on and off into sleep and tried to remain awake. Then out of nowhere came a voice. At first she thought she was dreaming, but then she recognized it as a voice of hope.

She left the ravine and started scrambling up the hill again, grabbing at small trees on the way to support herself and help push her further along till she reached the halfway point and stopped to listen for the sheriff's voice again. She'd know that voice anywhere! She knew he'd never leave her and just walk away with any finality. She cried in relief.

She tripped over a twig, pitched forward, fell, and began rolling a little back down the hill. She had to get to the crest of the hill in a hurry - the sheriff might leave if she didn't answer! She began to stumble her way back up to the top. She paused to catch her breath, staggered momentarily and fell flat on her face. She needed more energy to climb the hill again. She rose to her feet slowly and bound and determined even if she had to crawl, she pushed herself forward.

When she reached the halfway mark, she heard the voice again. "Jennifer, are you out there? Let me know where you are."

She couldn't catch her breath and lay down near the top of the hill.

Sheriff MacKenzie spoke softly, "Jennifer, where are you?"

She cried out, "God bless you, Sheriff! Here, Sheriff, over here!" She waved her hand in the air. His hand reached and stretched toward hers and she clasped it.

"Let me help you up, Jennifer."

"Oh, Sheriff, if you only knew how happy I am - YOU!" She was on her feet now.

"Hello, my love."

She pulled her hand free and ran down the hill back into the ravine. Michel was right behind her. She wrapped her arms around a small tree.

"You tricked me, you rat. What did you do with the sheriff - murder him?"

"How could you think me possible of doing such a vile thing?"

"I wouldn't put anything past you. Where's Sheriff MacKenzie?"

"Relax - I didn't touch him. Never got a chance to. For all I know he left the area like he said he would. Pretty good impersonation of the sheriff, if I say so myself, wouldn't you? Sure fooled you, my love. My versatility never ceases to amaze me. Now I got you and I'm not going to let you go.

"Stop playing games!" He grabbed her around the waist and tugged, pulling her free. Her fingers were bleeding. He alternately hauled and dragged her back up the hill.

"I'll never forgive you for this," she said, sniffling.

"You'll get over it in time. That was a rotten thing you did - kicking me."

"Look who's talking about being rotten."

She collapsed at the top of the hill.

"Come on, on your feet. We have to move and fast."

"Michel, please listen to me! If I promise you not to tell anyone, will you let me go?"

"Ha! Not good enough or as my alter ego Michel would say, 'Mon Dieu'."

"Don't you trust me?" Jenny asked.

"Under the present circumstances - no. Besides, I like the idea of running away with you where no one can find us. There's something romantic about such a flight, like an elopement."

"Well, I'm not going and you can't make me go."

"Oh yes, I can and will. Come on, get on your feet."

He began pulling her. "We got to get out of here before someone finds us."

"I can't move. I'm just too exhausted. Can't I rest a bit?"

"See how much energy you could have saved if you hadn't run away from me?"

"Listen," Michel said, "there's someone coming through."

Jennifer pricked up her ears, hoping it was the sheriff.

"Don't you dare say a word," Michel warned, jerking the gun out of his pocket.

He was a desperate man. For the first time since she knew him she felt fear for herself, tasted it in her mouth. What was he thinking about? What was going on in his head?

She never remembered seeing him so grim. What will happen if they're forced to spend the night here and then take off in the early morning hours? She'd never be able to get away. If only she had listened to the misgivings Mrs. Martin had uttered about Michel.

Michel pushed Jenny forward. "Come - let's get our horses and move out of here."

When they walked back to where the horses were tethered, there were no horses. "Whatever happened to them?" asked Jenny. "I know my horse would never have run away."

"The sheriff got them, I'm sure," Michel said. "All because of you. I can thank you for that."

"Why blame me? You're the outlaw, the fugitive! If you weren't, do you think the sheriff would have bothered to take the horses?"

"Well, if you hadn't led me on that merry chase, we'd have our horses already and could have left. Now we'll have to walk. It's going to be slow. Get a move on, you." He poked her with the gun.

"The sheriff and whoever is with him can easily overtake us any time now they want to. How are we ever going to get out of this place without the sheriff's knowledge? I wonder how many men he's got with him?"

Jenny knew the sheriff and his posse would never attack as long as Michel held her. If he used her as a shield, what then? She trembled at the thought.

"I didn't think the sheriff would just pick up and leave so easily, and now he knows, without the horses, we're stuck here for awhile."

"He had said he believed me about wanting to stay with you and he was leaving," said Jenny.

"That's the oldest trick in the book, my love. It never worked in the past and it won't work now."

"If the sheriff is here as you think, let me go and I promise I won't tell anyone where you are or where you've gone. Isn't that worth something to you?"

"Sorry, my love, but you're going with me and as soon as we get out of here, we're going to board a ship for France."

"But won't that make you a deserter, since you're still in the U.S. Army?"

"Jenny, you've got a lot to learn. I don't know what would be worse for me - to be tried as a deserter or a traitor or a murderer. That's another reason we're going to a friendly country like France: to escape."

They came to a clearing and stopped. "Isn't this where we met before?" Michel asked. "Sure, there's my toupee on the ground."

On the other side of the open space, the shrubbery suddenly stirred, followed by a swishing, then parted.

Michel pulled Jenny back into the bushes. "Duck down, duck down!" ordered Michel.

"Why?"

"Do as I say, dammit. Stop arguing with me. Do what I tell you to do." He pushed her head down, but she peeked through the foliage. The sheriff and Bert appeared.

"Sheriff, look at this," Bert said. "All these strips of hair. This is a moustache. Here are the remains of a beard. Very clever how Michel did that."

"All part of Michel's many disguises," the sheriff said. "Let's gather up these and save them for evidence."

"Why didn't I think of that?" Michel whispered to Jenny. "Now the sheriff can use that against me. I wonder where they took our horses. Keep your head down, Jenny; I'll tell you when it's clear."

"But without our horses, our progress will be slow," said Jenny.

"You leave those complex problems to me. I've worked them out before and I'll work them out now. We'll just stay in this spot for a few minutes until the sheriff and your friend Bert move on somewhere else."

Jenny began to weep.

"Stop that damn sniffling - I don't want any noise!"

Jenny looked at him. How could she not have seen the cruelty in his eyes in the past? Now that she was in his clutches, there seemed to be no avenue of escape open to her. She was cheered to know the sheriff and Bert were close by, and she wondered how many other men were around to help, too.

"Pay attention," Michel said. "They've apparently headed off in another direction. Let's move."

They walked slowly through the underbrush, taking care not to make any noise.

After awhile they stopped to rest. "Don't sit, stand. This is only a short stop."

Jenny peered through the shrubbery when she caught a glimpse of Bert coming from the opposite direction.

"That's Bert," she said excitedly.

"Shut up. That was Bert. I can pick him off easily right from here, so he'd never know what hit him." Michel raised the gun in his hand and took careful aim.

"Don't," Jenny said. "Please!"

"Give me one good reason why I shouldn't."

"He hasn't done anything to hurt you."

"He's searching for me so he can turn me over to the sheriff."

"Please, I beg of you," she said. "Please, don't! Leave him alone!"

"On one condition. Will you come with me now without making a fuss?"

"Yes, anything, but don't take his life."

"I think the best thing to do is to head back down the hill to that ravine area. We'll stay there, hidden till nightfall. They'll never find us."

"Then what happens at nightfall?"

"That's when we're going to get out of this hole."

"Bert," Sheriff MacKenzie said, "I want you to get on the other side of Michel and Jennifer. Don't do anything until I give the signal." The sheriff cupped his hands over his mouth. "Michel, drop your gun, we have you covered. You're surrounded so you might as well come peaceably."

Michel didn't respond.

"Why don't you answer him?" asked Jenny.

"Because I don't have to surrender to him or to anyone else. If I speak, then they'll be able to pinpoint exactly where we are and if the sheriff and his men move in on us, there'll be a gun battle and no one will survive. What do you think I should do?" asked Michel.

"Surrender."

"You got the wrong man. I don't surrender to anyone and that includes you."

Out of the corner of her eye, Jenny saw Bert. He looked right at her. Did he really see her?

"Put the gun away, Michel."

"Nothing doing. I want to see if I could really hit him from here." How can she distract Michel? Keep on talking.

"This time I won't miss," said Michel.

"Michel, don't, please." She stood on tiptoes and stretched her hands out to seize the gun, but he raised the gun higher, well beyond her reach.

Then Bert fired. The gun jumped out of Michel's hand, dropping to the ground, and they scrambled for the weapon, but Jenny got to it first and she pointed the gun at him.

"Now it's my turn," she said. "I told you I'd have the last word."

"Give me the gun," Michel said. "It will be better for both of us."

"I'm not going with you, Michel. I want to hear you agree to that."

"Not from my lips."

"Stay right where you are. Stay there," she screamed.

"Give me the gun." His hand was bleeding from Bert's shot. Then he lunged at her and she fired.

He fell to the ground. His body sprawled before her and she ran to him, kneeling beside him.

Half crying and sobbing, Jenny threw herself across Michel. "Michel, speak to me - I didn't mean to shoot you! Michel, forgive me - I didn't want to kill you! Forgive me, please! Don't die, Michel, please."

Bert and the sheriff ran towards her. Jenny threw herself in Bert's arms.

"I've killed him." Her sobs were uncontrollable.

"But if he attacked you and you had a gun, you probably shot him in self-defense," Bert said.

"It wasn't like that at all," said Jenny. "You shot the gun out of his hand."

"I know that," said Bert. "Sounds like self defense to me."

"No. He'd never hurt me, I know, and now I've killed him." She subsided in sobs.

The sheriff walked over to Michel, examining him. "Jennifer, he's not dead. He's got a superficial wound. We'll get him to the hospital and he'll be all right, well enough to stand trial. Where did you aim the gun?"

"I pointed at his knees. I was so frightened when he leaped at me I didn't know what to do, but I knew I didn't want to aim at this heart and kill him. But, Sheriff, why are his eyes closed?"

"Ir looks like when he fell, he hit his head on a good sized boulder. Come over here and I'll show you."

Jenny left the comfort of Bert's arms. She looked at Michel. "See," the sheriff said, "here's where the bullet entered his knee and then exited. Right here on the ground. He'll be all right, Jennifer. Don't worry about him."

"Bert," the sheriff said, "show Jennifer where the horses are and come back with Michel's horse. We'll lay him over the saddle and bring him into town."

"We've got the evidence against him, Jennifer. Bert and I searched his home. Found a lot of costumes there."

"For his roles in the play?"

"No, for his roles in the real world."

"Did you find the Confederate jacket with the missing button, too?"

"Sure did. One costume, though, stumped me - a priest's cassock."

"So that's who that was!" said Jenny.

"Did you know him? I mean, the priest?"

"When I was in the hospital, a priest came to call on me, to console me. Michel played that part very well. He was quite properly pious, but the only feature that was least priest-like was his insistent pumping me for information."

"What kind of information?"

"To see if I recognized my assailant; whether there was anything familiar to me about him."

"I can tie up all the details now for Todd's murder," the sheriff said. "Michel had the opportunity as the Duke of Clarence to kill Todd. The motive, of course, was to silence Todd because he caught him spying for the South."

"But what about Alice Tiernan's murder, Sheriff?"

"Michel has the diamond bracelet. I don't think we'll have too much trouble getting a confession from him."

"And the wagon train?" asked Jenny.

"You and Bert and Laura witnessed that holdup from the balloon, right?"

"But we didn't see his face."

"If we get the drop on his buddy, it won't be too hard to build a case against the both of them."

"Well, Sheriff, looks like you have everything wrapped up. You have the evidence and you have the motive and you have your prisoner."

"You're right, Jennifer."